Lisa, Lisa

Lisa, Lisa

Béatrice Shalit

Translated by David Kornacker

Available Press
Ballantine Books New York

An Available Press Book
Published by Ballantine Books
Translation copyright © 1992 by David Kornacker

Library of Congress Catalog Card Number: 91-76181
ISBN: 0-345-37339-1

Cover design by Barbara Leff
Cover illustration by André Yaniw
Text design by Holly Johnson

Manufactured in the United States of America

First American Edition: August 1992
10 9 8 7 6 5 4 3 2 1

Thanks to Tamar, who knows why

Lisa, Lisa

Sarah

The truth—"The whole truth and nothing but the truth, cross your heart and hope to die," my sister Lisa would insist when she was little—the *truth* is that I've had it up to here with my family. If I could trade them in, I would. Oh, not forever, but for a month, maybe even two. A kind of convalescence with normal people, the ones you see every day in the supermarket.

I'd choose a calm, placid husband with a big bushy mustache that completely covered his upper lip. He would spend the better part of his evenings putting together model airplanes in the basement of our house in the suburbs while I sat cable-stitching sweaters for my children, who would be watching a sitcom or the latest music videos without uttering a peep.

My father would live with us, but he wouldn't bother anyone, for he would be a full-fledged invalid, and just pushing his wheelchair around a little bit from time to time would be enough to keep him happy.

As for my sister . . .

"Sarah, why are you slowing down to pass that truck? It's dangerous. You should be accelerating."

"There, all you had to do was ask."

Suddenly the rain comes pouring down from the leaden sky, and even though I can barely see a thing, I jab at the accelerator to pass the truck. Shocked in all likelihood by my boldness, my traveling companion lets out a sigh. "No need to get angry, treasure."

"I'm sorry," I mumble. "I was daydreaming."

"I noticed. What about?"

I turn to scan my father's profile.

"About a week of R and R in the suburbs."

And since I am obviously not in the most stable of moods, he just nods and goes *mmm*.

I've driven the whole way. It's been raining nonstop ever since we left Paris, and my hands have cramped up from gripping the steering wheel so tightly. Leo did offer to trade off with me, but, wary of his annoying tendency to take himself for a Grand Prix racer, I flatly refused. Not only have I had it with my family—not the one from the supermarket, the *real* one, the one I'm stuck with—but I'm bored to tears by the prospect of spending two days in Anjou at the wedding of a girl I hardly know.

As I pull into a highway rest area, eyes burning with fatigue, my father checks his pocket watch, then draws his whiskey flask from one of the inner recesses of his coat. "I think it's that time of day, treasure," he declares, without specifying whether he is addressing the black leather flask or me. "Do you want some, or is it against your religion?"

Always the same jokes which, even today, in spite

4

of my exasperation, I accept with a smile of indulgence. He starts drinking at twelve o'clock sharp every day. But I adore Leo, and now that he is going to die, I am immersing myself in him, in the faint smell of alcohol that emanates from his clothes, in the special cadence of his voice, in his precise gestures, in his lively eyes whose vitality has not been diminished by the nearness of death. "Well, just a sip to raise my spirits. I'm going out for a smoke."

"Careful, you'll get cancer that way." He breaks out his short laugh, the one that sounds like a horse whinnying, then returns the flask to his lips.

Outside, on the trash-strewn grass, a little blonde girl is prancing around a German shepherd. Standing in the rain, I watch the child and the dog when it suddenly occurs to me that I have forgotten to remind Luc to give Miriam her Dramamine before they leave. The children insisted on making the trip with their father so they could break in his new station wagon, one of those huge cars I've always stubbornly refused to drive. Apparently it's a Ford, according to José. But José can't be trusted nowadays. When he comes out of his stupor, he'll say just about anything. I grind what's left of my cigarette into the mud and slip behind the wheel of the Austin, all the while thinking bitterly that I have every reason to be brokenhearted. My fifteen-year-old son is shooting heroin; my husband has left me—yes, left me, even if they do all claim that I really kicked him out; I haven't written a line in a year; and Leo has only a few months to live.

"How's José doing?"

"Not very well. Oh, you know perfectly well what the situation is, papa—a disaster. You can see him wasting away right before your eyes, and he won't hear of going into detox or anything like that. He says . . . he says he can kick the habit any time he wants. My little José, for God's sake! I'm simply devastated."

Leo gently smooths my hair the way he would when I was little. Then he murmurs, "To each generation its own. Mine was caught up in other things. What does Luc think?"

As a passing Ferrari comes dangerously close to hitting me, I shrug my shoulders. "I have no idea. Luc isn't saying a thing, as usual. It's a superhuman feat getting two words out of him. After all these years I still haven't learned how to interpret his silences."

"There's nothing to interpret, my dear. You're getting caught up in useless complications. Your husband is a man who doesn't talk much, that's all. Not everybody carries on like you and me. A little more whiskey?"

"Come on, not while I'm driving. And you, papa, you drink too much."

"Now that I don't have to worry about my health, I don't see why I should deprive myself."

Hearing his words, I suppress an annoyed sigh. If he makes one more reference to his death, I'm turning around and going back. What an absurd idea, dragging us all to the marriage of his friend Paul's niece. He called each of us in one by one, Miriam included, poor

6

little thing, to implore us to come to Echards, Paul's château, on what would surely be his last trip. A family reunion, he explained with a certain irony. Not even Luc had the presence of mind to get out of it.

"Don't look at me like that, treasure. I'm expected up in Jew Heaven."

"Please, Leo, stop it. I've had enough of your morbid allusions. I can't take any more of them. Think of me a little, the one who's going to be left behind with nothing but her memories." Fighting back tears, I tighten my grip on the steering wheel.

"Okay, Sarah, no more doom and gloom. Look, we're coming into Angers. Can't be more than half an hour from here. Just enough time to tell you a secret."

"A secret? Oh no! Please not that, not today."

"As you wish," replies my father.

A mischievous sparkle brightens his green eyes. Having just stopped at an intersection, I cast a glance at him and cannot help asking, "Well?"

"I was sworn to silence, but for you I'll gladly break my vow. You look so tense today. It's about José."

Since he's been sick, Leo's Russian accent has grown slightly more pronounced; it's as if he were returning to the land of his birth. "José," I sigh. "Have you seen him recently?"

He is silent for a moment before answering. "Yes, he stopped in to see me a few days ago."

"To ask you for money, I suppose. He must need it."

My father shakes his head. His smile is positively beatific. Softly he replies, "Not at all."

"Then I don't understand. Why did he come to you?"

"He wanted to talk to me. And you know what? I guessed his secret just as he was about to confess it."

I run an inquisitive eye over his cheeks, now somewhat hollowed by his disease. "I'm warning you," I tell him curtly. "Right now I can't tolerate hearing about some new disaster."

Indifferent to my exasperation, he beams triumphantly. "Calm down, Sarah, and listen carefully. Your son isn't taking any drugs. This shooting-up of his is all an act."

I am so surprised that the Austin swerves.

"What is this nonsense? He's taken you in, that's all."

"It's the truth, treasure. He's gotten tangled up in his story and doesn't know how to get himself untangled."

At the very moment he finishes his sentence, the Austin sputters to a stop. Out of gas as usual. When I travel by car, I always check the oil a hundred times before I leave but never think to fill the tank. "Excuse me, Leo, I'm getting more and more absentminded. The kids gave me a gas can for Christmas. It must be somewhere in the trunk. You'd better wait here while I go look for a service station. I'm going to push the car over to the side of the road."

"Let me help you, Sarah," my father offers as he throws back his frail shoulders.

"I don't want you to wear yourself out."

"Don't worry, treasure. I still have some strength left."

The rain has practically stopped, and a pale sun is beginning to emerge between the clouds. Before setting out on foot, gas can in hand, I deposit a kiss on Leo's cheek and whisper, "Thank you for telling me José's secret."

Striding briskly, I think about the rotten trick my son has played on me. It was certainly naïve of me to have believed for even one single minute that he had turned into a junkie practically overnight.

Some of the trees are already in bloom, and my bad mood gradually dissipates. Maybe Leo will pull through after all. By the time the attendant has filled my gas can, I'm already imagining our weekend in Angers with a bit less dread.

Paul, Leo's fellow captive from the old days, loves to play host to us. They're quite a pair, those two. There's nothing quite so overwhelming as listening to them recounting, without excess emotion, stories about the concentration camp they escaped together. As a souvenir of that time, each of them still has a number on his forearm. One, my father, is Jewish; the other is not.

I can still hear Paul's determined voice resounding over the telephone the other day. "I won't let some lousy little tumor take your father. Believe me, Sarah, I'll get him out of this."

Unable to say anything in reply, I had started to cry while Leo's faithful comrade went on shouting. "A life like his can't be cut short by this bloody nonsense. So, I'll be expecting the whole lot of you on Saturday. And don't you dare get any ideas about backing out. I've got a surprise for you."

Choking back my tears, I had managed to say, "Paul, I'll come. I promise."

"That's better. Not interested in my surprise, though?"

"No, no, of course I am."

"We have a visitor here with us. A charming young man, very bright, who's had the most amazing thing happen to him. He suddenly lost his memory after being in an automobile accident. I thought that as a novelist, you would find his case intriguing."

I then remembered that Paul was in the habit of taking rather strange people into his home. "For the moment, I've stopped writing, Paul. Circumstances beyond my control. My imagination has run dry."

"It will come back, my dear. Nothing is forever in this world. Soon you'll be making up new stories again. Believe me, I have confidence in you. Keep the faith and see you Saturday."

Yes, in spite of my many worries, I am thrilled at the prospect of again seeing Paul, whose regular appearances during my childhood punctuated my life in our home on rue La Bruyère.

In the distance, a stoop-shouldered old man standing near the car is shielding his eyes from the sun as he looks at the ramparts of the château d'Angers. When I shout "Papa," he turns and smiles at me.

José

Sometimes I just crack up when I think how I almost got named Jeremiah, after the Old Testament prophet, a real bullshit artist according to Leo. And he's read the Bible in Hebrew.

"That was a close call," my grandfather told me with a chuckle. "You wouldn't have been much fun weighed down by such a name. That distinctive imagination of yours would have ended up buried in the depths of what some fools pretentiously call your soul, when all they really mean is your consciousness."

For once mom ended up agreeing with her whole entourage, a group made up of her husband, her father, her sister, and certain close friends. Anyway, she gave up on that deadly name Jeremiah. She still wanted to stick with the letter *J*, however, and apparently spent a whole day pondering the matter before announcing that my name was to be José, a name inspired by both bullfighting and light opera. Anyway, I can't complain, seeing as I avoided the worst, and whenever my mother murmurs "my José" in that clear, soft voice of hers, I'd willingly go get her ten of those chocolate bars with hazelnuts that she likes so much.

Things have been a mess at home for about six

months now. Beginning of September, the first day of school no less, my father packed his bags. Patience isn't exactly his long suit.

"I've got to get out of here," he said loudly. "You can't even think straight in this nuthouse."

Mom took him at his word and, hands trembling with rage, showed him the door. It's true that with us, things are always a little crazy, but personally I like it that our apartment is so lively. On a typical day Aunt Lisa might be playing four-handed piano pieces with Miriam, my little brat of a sister, to accompany the central European folk songs the two of them are belting out while Leo is noisily making pirogis in the kitchen and the stereo is going full blast so mom can listen to her blues albums while she's shut up in her study writing.

But now that my old man's jumped ship, she's fallen into this weird daze. She's forgotten about the novel she was working on; mornings, instead of talking with us the way she used to, she sits there stirring her coffee and staring off into space—she barely notices we're around. I'm an easygoing guy who can get used to most anything, but I can't stand not being able to make my mom laugh any more. Even Leo's coming up short in that area, and God knows he knocks himself out trying. But she just stares at us with this sad, empty look on her face—you can tell her mind is full of gloomy thoughts. Me and my grandfather came up with one hell of a plan to cheer her up, but it didn't work. Jokes that would normally make her laugh have been leaving her stone cold. Even her sister Lisa, who's usually full of ideas, is at the end of her rope. And while Miriam, who couldn't care less about the gloomy atmosphere at home, has been calmly going on with her little girl life, I've been sweating blood trying to figure out what to do. I kept thinking that mom had to get excited about something, and I had an idea. Since I couldn't make her laugh any more, I'd make her cry. When I told my buddy Ludo the plan, he just rolled his eyes.

"Your story is such a bunch of crap. If your mother's feeling down now, she's just going to feel worse. No, what she needs to cheer her up is a man."

"A man!" I shouted. "What would she do with a man?"

We were hanging out in the schoolyard just before physics class. Ludo started snickering. "Want me to draw you a picture, Joey boy?"

Ludo knows perfectly well that first of all, I hate being called Joey, and that if there's one thing I can't stand, it's the idea of some man in bed with my mother. "You're an asshole," I shot back, then turned and walked away.

"Hey, don't get all bent out of shape!" he called after me, but I didn't say a word to him for two solid days.

Me, I was making sure everything was ready. Getting supplies was no big deal. All I had to do was buy a few syringes from a pharmacist who didn't know us. It was the other part of my plan that ended up being

14

tougher. Pretending to be a junkie when the mere mention of drugs makes you want to puke is really rough. I must have a talent for acting, because the minute mom saw me dragging around the apartment with a nasty look on my face, she came out of hibernation, and the questions came pouring down on me at a frantic pace. Then one Sunday she said to me in her normal tone of voice, "I'd like to have a word with you alone, José. Come into my study where we won't be disturbed."

She sat down on her side of the desk and gave me a worried look. "So, do you have anything to tell me?" she asked.

I slowly counted to ten before answering dully, "No, mom, nothing special."

"Things going okay at school?"

Slumping listlessly, I answered, "Yeah, yeah. Same as ever."

As a matter of fact, I get good grades. I grind away at my own pace, and it's not like tenth grade is going to be too much for me. I do extremely well in math, physics, and history, and that's a fact; as for the rest, I make out all right.

Since it's not my style to say two words and clam up—usually I'm quite the talker—mom stared at me intently, her yellow-green eyes bright with worry. All the same, it was a step in the right direction. These last few months her eyes had been dead; they didn't have that warm glow any more, the one that's made me feel better so many times.

"Tell me, José, are you upset about your father moving out?"

"No," I answered sincerely. "Now there's no one here to yell at us when things get too crazy around the apartment."

She nervously lit a cigarette, and a heavy silence settled over the room. "José," she finally said in a trembling voice, "I saw syringes in the top drawer of your dresser. You know I wouldn't normally go snooping around, but lately you've been acting so strangely—I had to find out what was going on. This could be the plot for one of my books—a teenager gets hooked on drugs, his family falls apart—but I never would have dreamed it could happen to you. Oh, José, you've always been so friendly, so bright, so happy! A perfect child, everybody used to say."

A single tear ran down her left cheek. She shivered slightly, then looked out the window. "Surely it's my fault," she murmured in an even more pitiful voice than the one Miriam uses when she's in the middle of one of her serious pouts.

Well, I admit I almost broke down and told her everything. Ever since I was little, mom and I have had an easy time talking to each other. With my sister it's another story. Most of the time, they have to communicate through me or Leo. The two of them live in a constant state of war interrupted by the odd cease-fire.

But to get back to my visit to mom's study: I was

on the verge of admitting that smack really wasn't my thing, when it occurred to me that I was much happier with her making all this fuss over me instead of moping on account of my father. I had to go on with my act until she got dad's leaving off her mind.

"Do you have any idea what we're going to do?"

Her tuneful voice brought me back down to earth. I stared at the painting behind her head, a nineteenth-century Russian seascape, and let the words tumble slowly out of my mouth. "Don't get all worked up, mom. I'm gonna clean up my act. Besides, I'm only taking two doses a day, y'know."

She didn't know at all. Neither did I, for that matter. In our family, we think of aspirin as a hard drug. Out of the corner of my eye, I watched her mouth tremble as I contemplated my own shortcomings on the linguistic front. I should have said *shooting up* twice a day, not *taking two doses* a day.

Looking me straight in the eye, she suddenly said, "Tell me . . . I get this funny feeling listening to you. And you certainly look healthy enough. Maybe this is wishful thinking on my part, but are you sure you're not making some of this up?"

I had forgotten mom's sixth sense. When you try to put one over on her, she goes along for a while—a complete sucker—and just when you're telling yourself she's fallen for it, she wrinkles her forehead, her eyes go all cloudy, and she exclaims, "Why, you're lying to me."

"No, mom," I answered, slouching farther down in the chair and putting on my most apathetic look. "I don't have enough, y'know, imagination for something like that. Hey, like, I wish, but this is no b.s. Just ask Ludo. He knows what's up."

"Ludo too! He's? . . . No, no, that's just not possible. He'd faint at the mere sight of a syringe."

"Not Ludo, mom, just me."

"Well," she said with a hint of her usual irony, "I'll simply have to get used to having a junkie in the family. I'm going to talk to your father about it. He'll be positively ecstatic. He'll say that I don't know how to raise you kids, which is probably true." Then she added coldly, "You may go now, José, our little talk is over."

That all happened exactly three weeks ago. I mention this particular detail because it's important. The day after my confrontation with mom, I told Ludo everything at the Switchblade, the café across the street from school. He listened to my story, then shrugged his shoulders. "Pal, your problem is that you love your mother too much," he said.

"Yeah, you like her a little too. When you stop by the apartment, it's not me you're coming to see, it's her. You cling to her like a leech."

He turned away, trying to hide his flushed cheeks. "Okay," he admitted, "she's not like everyone else. She's got a certain charm, or something like that. Then again, I'm not her son. Hell, I'm surprised you're not

18

a faggot by now. Anyway, that's your business. But what about this big act of yours? How long are you planning to keep it up? Because if you ask me, you're heading for trouble."

"We'll just see about that," I replied.

Walking home that day, I felt an overwhelming sense of shame. Why invent a story like this to snap mom out of her bad mood? Basically, my plan was worthless, a realization I had confirmed for me when I ran right into my grandfather Leo in the courtyard of our building. Now Leo's a pretty short guy, but generally speaking he stands up ramrod straight with his chest thrown out and his clothes looking just so. Only this time his shoulders were slumped forward, his tie was hanging out of his vest, and, strangest of all, instead of having his usual healthy complexion, he was completely pale.

"Hi, Leo," I called out, pretending not to notice his condition.

"Kid," he said right back, "I always thought I had guts, but I just found out I was wrong."

After that rather mysterious pronouncement, he grabbed onto the banister and started trudging up the stairs. I followed behind, wondering what could have upset him so much. When we got to the door, he stopped to catch his breath and gave me a piercing stare. "So you're taking drugs?"

"Aww grandpa . . ." I mumbled, caught off guard.

He shook his head, then said, "Your mother's worried, which must make you happy. But *I* don't believe it. Doesn't take a crystal ball to spot a cock-and-bull story like yours. I know you better than anyone. Come see me tomorrow, José. You know full well that whatever you tell me, I won't pass judgment on you. Come on," he added, reverting to his demoralized tone, "I have something to tell all of you."

Once we were inside the apartment, he asked me to get him a big glass of ice water. Then, in a slightly strained voice, he called mom and Miriam over.

"Lisa isn't here?"

"Leo," replied my mother, "Lisa is an adult; she doesn't come here every day. Besides, right now she's involved with her new fiancé."

Mom calls the horde of guys Lisa shacks up with her fiancés. By profession, Lisa is an astrophysicist, but when it comes to choosing men, she's no rocket scientist.

"Gather round, children, and shut off that god-awful music, Miriam—I feel too old for that kind of racket today."

Grandpa settled in his usual place, the leather easy chair in the living room, took a few sips from his flask, and stared in the general direction of one of the windows. Silently huddled around him, we were all waiting to hear whatever it was he was planning to tell us.

"Are you sick, grandpa?" asked my little sister.

Leo let out a sigh that sounded like a sob.

"I just got back from seeing Citrus."

"Dr. Citrus told me that I could eat ice cream whenever I have a sore throat," trumpeted Miriam.

The person we call Citrus—that was his code name during the resistance—is Leo's oldest friend. They agitated together back when they were communists.

"Well?" Mom asked in a whisper, her eyes suddenly dark with worry.

"So," Leo replied as he stroked Miriam's tangled hair, "my liver's affected—shot to pieces. It's cancer, kids, cancer. Inoperable. He gives me three or four months to . . . well, to live. Not much, is it? I still have so many books to read, so many new places to see. Don't cry, Sarah, my little darling."

Mother jumped up and clasped Leo's hands tightly in hers.

"Maybe Citrus made a mistake," she said. "You have to go see another doctor, someone who doesn't know that you drink day and night."

Miriam was hugging her knees to her chest and saying over and over, "But I don't want you to die, grandpa."

I didn't want him to die either. My heart was going a hundred miles an hour, and the lump in my throat was so big I couldn't make a sound. I had been putting on this stupid junkie act to shake mom up and here a real disaster had come our way. I couldn't even imagine life without Leo.

It got dark, but no one thought to turn on the lights. I looked at the three of them one by one: Miriam curled up in a ball, mom kneeling against the leather easy chair, grandpa leaning toward her and probably thinking about his impending death. I swore to myself that from then on, no matter what happened, I would do my best to do the right thing, just the way Leo had his whole life long.

Sarah

At the entrance to the tree-lined driveway, the little stream where José learned to fish is cloaked in white chestnut blossoms. Wearing a cap borrowed from his grandfather, he would sit next to Luc for hours without making a sound, something quite remarkable for such a talkative child. This was back when we used to come down often with the children to visit Paul. We were certainly a very boisterous family, but we were also a very happy one and seemed destined to stay together forever.

Even as a small child, I dreaded endings. The end of a party, the end of childhood, the end of love . . . To keep from suffering, I tend to make the first move and bring things to a head myself. Throughout the trying discussions that led up to our breakup, Luc would never look me in the eye. Whenever I would try to talk to him, he would either focus on something behind me or read the paper. I came to feel I had become some sort of particularly cumbersome burden for him. Is it possible that he doesn't love me at all any more? He used to call me "my little kitten" in such a tender voice. As usual when I know I'm going to have to see him, my mouth is dry and my stomach tied up in knots.

"Look, Sarah," exclaims Leo, "they're here already."

At the far end of the driveway near the château, Luc's new station wagon is sparkling in the sun. Looking tiny in her red dress, a little girl with medium-length brown hair comes running up to us. "Mommy, grandpa, Zaza came in the car with us. We played twenty questions and dad made up a song. 'Those Abner girls are really tough, they never quit when things get rough. Pottier men are really neat, 'cause they've got the biggest feet.' Then it goes . . ."

"Say goodbye to Leo Abner, 'cause he's gonna die of cancer," Leo interrupts. "That rhymes too."

Miriam covers her ears vigorously and says, "Grandpa, can't you ever talk about anything else? I'm sick of hearing about you and your cancer. I cried all the way here. So did Zaza."

Miriam has always called her aunt Zaza. Her first word was Zaza, not mama. At the time, I was terribly jealous of Lisa. Even now, I envy her patience with my children. Maybe it's my fault for having overprotected her, but whatever the reason, my sister never really stopped being an adolescent. Her narrow face, almond-shaped green eyes, and slender figure combine to make her look like a schoolgirl. She's never wanted to get married and start a family, supposedly because she's convinced that World War III is just around the corner.

Even if she thinks she's being sincere, I know she's not telling the whole truth. My sister has very strange relationships with men. She collects them like butterflies, then tires of them the moment their shimmering colors fade.

Reaching over the rolled-down car window, I take my daughter's warm little hands in mine and squeeze them affectionately.

"Come on, Sarah, pull forward," shouts Leo, "we're not going to stay parked here all weekend. Look at the frantic way poor old Paul is waving at us over there."

"Listen, papa, I have the right to take a break, don't I? You think I like the idea of this little family reunion? Frankly, I'd have preferred to stay home. At this rate, I'm gonna send you on to the afterlife myself. Straight to hell."

"Calm down, treasure. Everything will be fine. You'll see."

After applying a kiss to Miriam's wrist, I drive the Austin slowly up the driveway and park it near the other cars. When my father said "Everything will be fine," it was no doubt in reference to his son-in-law—he's always had a soft spot in his heart for Luc. Like so many others, Luc was all but bewitched by my father from the very first.

As a matter of fact, it was right here at Echards, in this very Angevin château, that we all met. Marianne, Paul's wife, was living here with her brothers, and one of the family's countless cousins was getting married on the grounds. I spent the whole night wondering about the young man with blond hair, slightly slanting eyes, and a gleaming smile who kept following my father around. As we sat down to dinner, each group of guests at its own little table, Lisa whispered to me, "That guy talking to daddy looks good enough to eat. I'm going to join them." Thinking that the young stranger had a certain charm myself, I followed my little sister. He was short and stocky with a very round face and a look that exuded a sort of sweetness bordering on innocence. As the years went by, I saw him conceal that sweetness and bury it deep within himself as if it were some dirty secret to be hidden away at all costs. Anyway, when Leo broke off the conversation that first time and introduced Luc to his daughters, he barely looked at us.

After that wedding, he got into the habit of visiting Leo regularly at our place on rue La Bruyère. One night Lisa ran out of patience and seized the offensive. "I'm stealing Luc from you and taking him to the movies," she declared. My father's latest protégé nodded his consent, then glanced mischievously in my direction and added, "That's fine as long as Sarah comes along." I forget what movie we went to see that night, but I'll always remember the furious look my sister shot my way. In the darkness of the movie theatre he took my hand, and that's the way it all started. . . .

Our host is stamping about impatiently at the foot

of his front porch. He lays his hands on his old comrade's shoulders, then embraces him warmly, tears shining in his eyes. "Ah, Leo, here you are at last. What funny stories have you been saving up for me this time?"

"A few, comrade, a few. Just give me a minute. Ah, I've got one. There's this Jewish pedlar, and all his life he's saved everything he makes. His clothes are threadbare, his socks are full of holes, the soles of his shoes have worn through . . . you get the picture. Anyway one day he decides to stop working and live off his savings. He goes to the most expensive store in town and buys himself magnificent suits, fine Oxford dress shirts, cashmere ties—the works. Then he picks out a four-star restaurant for dinner. As he's leaving the restaurant, a car runs him over. So when he gets to Heaven, he finds God and he says, 'God, how could you do this to me?' And God says: 'But I didn't recognize you.'"

I've heard this joke at least twenty times and can't help groaning, but Paul breaks out in warm, hearty laughter, then deposits a kiss on my forehead. "I'm touched that you all decided to come, Sarah. But don't act too crazy this time. I have cataclysmic memories of your last visit to Echards. Living alone has turned me into a fussy old bachelor."

Paul's wife died three years ago of a heart attack. Leo proclaimed that his friend would never get over it, but Paul is a force of nature. He came out of retirement and went back to practicing commercial law. Lisa and I often gush over the way friendship has united a blue-blooded aristocrat and a self-taught Jewish sweater maker.

"We'll be good as gold, Paul. I promise."

"I just had a long talk with Miriam," Paul continues. "She told me that if I ever get bored, all I have to do is come live with you. Apparently your children give you no trouble at all. They certainly look as if they have their heads screwed on straight."

"If you only knew!" I sigh, and Leo flashes a brief smile.

I scan the edge of the front lawn, looking in vain for any sign of Lisa or Luc; off in the distance, however, I can make out José playing soccer with a stranger. Maybe it's the guy who's lost his memory. José notices that I'm watching him and waves to me, then exchanges a few words with the stranger and walks up to us, his hands in his pockets.

"Grandpa," he shouts, "I'll bet mom pulled the old empty gas tank trick on you. She's got a real flair for that one."

"Indeed she did, but I showed remarkable patience," replies Leo, then adds in an undertone for my benefit: "Be gentle with him."

Gentle! I feel more like slapping him across the face a few times. How could I have believed for even a second that José was hooked on drugs? His rosy cheeks and dark shining eyes positively radiate health.

"You know, José, you aren't standing on such firm ground to be making fun of me. I feel like taking a walk. How 'bout coming along. Do you mind, Paul?"

"Sarah, my home is your home—do as you like."

"Can I come too?" asks Miriam.

José shoots me a vaguely sheepish look as I answer, "No, dear, I have something to talk over with your brother."

"Oh that! I know all about it," shouts my little daughter. "Daddy told Zaza the whole story in the car. But I wasn't asleep. He said, 'The latest news is that José is shooting drugs.' "

Miriam doesn't know how to talk in a normal voice; she always screams at the top of her lungs. And while Paul is standing there wide-eyed, she solemnly mimics sticking a syringe into her forearm.

"And what did José have to say?" asks an intrigued Paul.

"He said it wasn't true."

Miriam's shrill voice is still echoing around the grounds as I drag my son away from the front door of the château.

"Mom," he mumbles, "I don't feel like talking about it right away."

I shrug my shoulders and we walk on. After a few moments of silence he asks, "Was it the same when you were a kid and used to come here?"

"Exactly the same. I have a vivid memory of our first visit. Everything seemed too big, I felt completely lost. Lisa had chicken pox and cried the whole time. I don't know if it was because she was sick or because your grandmother had just left us."

"I don't get it, mom. Why did she cut out on the three of you like that?"

"It's complicated. While your grandfather was in the camps, she met another man. Many years later she decided to join him in America. Everyone was so drawn to Leo's aura that she may have felt lonely and unloved. Overshadowed, I guess."

"To the point of deserting her daughters?"

"I don't know, José. I was only six years old. I hated her for a long time. Lisa used to ask Leo, 'What's my mommy like?' and I would put my hands over my ears so I wouldn't hear anything."

We come up to the barn, the place where I spent so much time sprawled in the hay crying over my mother's disappearance. She had embraced each of us one morning at dawn—it was still dark outside—then disappeared. José bashfully presses my arm and says, "Don't worry, mom. We love you."

The letters from America used to come regularly— once a week. Leo would read them aloud, trying to sound casual, but at times his voice would tremble so badly it became inaudible. Fascinated, Lisa would hang on his every word while I stood with my arms folded across my chest, watching them and cursing the woman to whom I bore such a strong resemblance—same color eyes, same color hair, same high cheekbones and broad mouth—swearing to myself that I would never forgive her. And then one day when I was twenty years old, I gave in to an irresistible urge to see the woman who had brought me into this world. And I flew to Chicago.

"Oh, my José, she loved us in her own way. I figured that out much later when I saw her again. The walls of her little apartment in Chicago were plastered with picures of us—her daughters. She had kept all sorts of things that had once been ours: handkerchiefs, baby clothes, stuffed animals . . . anything. It was very sad."

Upon my return, I had tried to tell my sister of our mother's despair, of how this woman's beauty had been eaten away by sorrow, but this time it was Lisa's turn to refuse to listen.

As I sit on the grass in front of the barn with José kneeling beside me, I suddenly wonder if Leo didn't feel inordinately proud of himself for raising us alone, for exposing us to culture and keeping us entertained after his own fashion.

"You want me to explain it all to you, mom?"

What's he talking about? Oh yes, his secret! Syringes, drugs, and so forth. I answer in measured tones, "I suppose I understand. You thought I wasn't paying enough attention to you, right?"

His profile stands out in sharp relief against the sun as he breaks a stick over his knee. "Well, yes and no. What bothered me the most was seeing you wander around like a zombie. Hell, you never laughed any more."

I promised myself I'd stay calm, but in spite of my

best intentions, I can feel the anger boiling up inside me, and when I open my mouth, I'm practically shouting. "I didn't laugh any more! C'mon José, was that really a reason to fabricate something so horrible? How could a bright kid like you do such a thing?"

"Mom, don't get all upset! They can hear you a mile away."

"I don't give a damn. Do you know that I even went to see your math teacher, Monsieur Carreau?"

"Caillaux, mom."

"Fine, Carreau, Caillaux, whatever. Anyway, he at least got a good laugh out of the whole thing. He said, 'If that José of yours is taking drugs, I'm quitting teaching and going into import-export.' I hope your father gave you hell in the car."

José rolls his eyes when he hears that, and I smile in spite of myself. Luc can get awfully worked up when he loses his temper.

"He certainly didn't hold back. What a nightmare of a trip. Not that he was fooled or anything. When I said it wasn't true, he calmed down right away and said he knew perfectly well it wasn't. Look, mom, there he is. I'm warning you, if you two start yelling at each other, I'm out of here."

In his black sweatshirt and jeans, Luc looks like a very young man from a distance. He ambles up to us nonchalantly, but as always since we've separated, he obstinately refuses to meet my gaze.

"Hello," we mumble at the same time in that kind of neutral tone one uses with strangers.

José stares at his feet, embarrassed at finding himself caught between his parents.

"Sarah," Luc says cautiously, "your father felt a little dizzy. Nothing serious, but he had to lie down."

Terrified, I jump up and, as I start running toward the house, behind me I hear him sigh, "Poor Leo."

Luc

When I wake up at night next to a woman who doesn't breathe in a familiar way, whose skin doesn't feel familiar, and who doesn't have a familiar scent, I'm wracked with nostalgia at the thought that I've lost Sarah. If I could cry, I would sob uncontrollably, but something in the pit of my stomach holds back the tears, and I lie perfectly still in the darkness, overwhelmed by sadness.

I left because her unforgiving gaze reflected an intolerable image of myself back to me, the image of a person who's weak, indecisive, violent, and above all tiny, not just physically—how many times have the children said with cruel innocence, "Mommy's taller than you are, daddy"?—but emotionally. It's as if Sarah Abner's heart held emotions that calmly take in the entire universe: extraterrestrials, mutants, prehistoric creatures, and who knows what all else included. I left her up on her throne, the one that belongs to her as a writer of intelligence whose works have a certain special tone created through a subtle mixing of irony and sensitivity, works that aroused my most fervent admiration until the day I realized that my sole function was to serve as her Majesty's court jester, and not a very amusing one at that.

During the day I don't think about her. In fact, I work so hard that I don't have time to concentrate on anything else, and certainly none to dedicate to introspection, that useless mental exercise she excoriates me for not practicing. At night, I go out or I fuck—what a relief to use that word, a word that, despite her supposed tolerance, she would find disgusting—especially whenever I got angry with her for the very fact that she *wouldn't* fuck. But during the course of my sleepless nights, a stabbing pain I can't ignore awakens within me—the memory of the woman I loved so much.

Paul, whose family is related to mine, was the first to tell me about the Abners. I thought nothing of it at the time, for much as he made frequent references to the Jewish comrade with whom he had escaped Bergen-Belsen, I had no idea what that renowned Leo's last name was. This was in July 1970. On my way back from a term studying architecture in Venice, I spent a few days with my parents in Angers and dropped by the château to say hello to Paul and Marianne.

"So you'll be coming to Agnes' wedding next week," Marianne had said. "You know the one I mean—the youngest Moreau girl, a little round thing who likes to ride horses. Don't you remember? She had a crush on you, Luc."

"Come now, Marianne," Paul had protested amiably. "This boy has no sense of family, to use your favorite expression. I see by the baffled look on his face that he has absolutely no idea who you're talking about. But you're going to come anyway, Luc; I'd like you to meet the Abners."

"The Abners," I echoed. "Judging by the name, they're not exactly family either."

Paul's kindly eyes hardened a bit. "No, of course not," he replied, "but if it were up to me, I wouldn't think twice about trading all of those irritating cousins of ours for Leo Abner and his daughters."

I'm not exactly sure why, but I had always imagined Leo as a single man—no wife, no children. "I'd be very happy to meet your friend, Paul," I murmured politely. "You've told me so much about him over the years."

"Yes, well, Leo is an exceptional man. If it weren't for him, I never would have made it back alive. Just wait until you see his daughters. The younger one, Lisa, is a flitty little blonde with an angelic face and green eyes like a Persian cat. As for the older one . . . well, you'll see for yourself."

"Luc has such exotic tastes," remarked Marianne between sips of her afternoon cocktail, "that even the Abner girls may seem a bit plain to him."

The summer before, I had shocked, nay horrified, my family by bringing with me to Echards a woman black as ebony from the Ivory Coast. Not that my family was truly racist, just constrained by a very strict clan mentality.

"Paul, you're not really planning to push me into

the arms of one of your friend's daughters, are you? That sort of thing never works with me. The minute I start hearing how great some woman is, I get an allergic reaction at the mere thought of her."

"Yes, yes, we'll see. For the moment just agree to come to dinner."

By the night of that infamous wedding, I had forgotten all about the Abner sisters. My week had been turned upside down by a series of endless phone conversations between me and a woman I wasn't in love with who kept accusing me of treating her inconsistently, an accusation I'd heard before and was to hear again. It was as if all the women in my life expected me to be chatty as a parrot and hard as a rock.

Champagne glass in hand, I was traipsing from one cousin to the next when I suddenly found myself standing two feet away from her. She was leaning against one of the walls of the hunting lodge and clumsily dragging on a cigarette after the fashion of someone smoking for the first time. A mound of dark red hair framed her angular face and high cheekbones. When she more or less mechanically gazed my way, I noticed that her eyes were a remarkable sort of golden-yellow color with a hint of green. Was she beautiful? Even today I couldn't say, but in any event she certainly didn't look like anyone else. I think it was there at the wedding of that little cousin whose name I didn't even remember that I fell instantly in love with Sarah, even though I had a premonition that I was drowning. I was listening absentmindedly to one of my uncles tell me about Venice when Paul grabbed me by the arm. "Excuse me, Robert, but I'm kidnapping your nephew," he said over his shoulder with his usual spontaneity as he dragged me toward the château. "So tell me," he added with a laugh, "have you had your allergic reaction yet? I was watching you back there a few minutes ago. You looked positively spellbound."

"Don't get carried away," I replied meditatively. "I suppose she's the older Abner girl, the one you didn't describe. What's her name?"

"Sarah. A most regal name, don't you think? Come on, I'll introduce you to Leo."

I'm the only one of my cousins to have gone on to college for an advanced degree, a fact that has earned me something of a reputation for being an intellectual and a great deal of affection from Paul, whose judgments can be quite harsh. For my part, I've always sought out the company of this man of intelligence and integrity who played an important part in the Resistance to boot, a man I would have secretly liked to have had for a father.

Sitting at the dining room table was a thickset man whose white tuxedo looked a bit tight in the shoulders. He was slumped forward with his elbows resting heavily on the table and his chin propped in his hands—a pose I was to discover to be a favorite of his. What first struck me about Leo was the great liveliness of his frank gaze.

"Well, well, if it isn't your protégé, the famed Luc,"

Leo exclaimed with a smile. "Sit down across from me so we can talk. I hate polite chitchat, and people my own age bore me to tears—they're all so monotonous, so unwilling to live up to their dreams. Here, Luc, have a sip of my magic potion."

He pushed a black leather flask my way. "And just what is this potion of yours?"

"Whiskey. Come on, try it, you'll see. It's got a bit more zip than champagne."

His voice was warm, almost sensual. After introducing me to whiskey that first time, Leo went on to tell me, in no particular order, about American movies, which he loved; the crimes of Stalin; the war in Vietnam; French food—"one big joke, and when it comes to pastry, they all ought to go to Vienna for lessons"; boxing, his favorite sport; and human beings in general: "Every person has something of value to offer, and that something is always a surprise." As I listened, I noticed that this man exuded a peculiar mix of exceptional strength and practically feminine charm. On occasion his rambling sentences would bear the slightest trace of a foreign accent, a sort of singsong intonation.

With the help of the liquor, I, in turn, began waxing lyrical about my studies in Italy, the beauty of Venetian palaces, and I don't know what all else. His head tilted slightly to one side, Leo listened to me with phenomenal concentration, and I remember that thanks to him my doubts about my future suddenly evaporated that night, for Leo possesses the well-nigh unique gift of bestowing intelligence upon the person who's talking to him. When he stood up, I was surprised to discover that he was shorter than I.

At dinner, his daughters joined us. As Paul had indicated, Lisa was bright, lively, and very pretty, but I got the impression that her apparent happiness was a cover for the fact that something was missing from her life, or even for some wound she had suffered. As for Sarah, I did my best not to look at her. She was more reserved. Ah, that famed reserve. Naturally I didn't know at the time that it masked her driving ambition. She doesn't have a mean bone in her body, but she's utterly indifferent to anything that doesn't have to do with her writing or her family. I'm being unfair, actually; Sarah loves children, adolescents, and certain women. But much as she would never come right out and say it, no man ever finds favor in her eyes. She would probably claim to have loved me, but the day I stopped amusing her, she withdrew into her writing—and the apartment became a kind of Abner reservation where there was no longer any room for me, a man named Luc Pottier.

The famous morning three weeks ago when Sarah phoned, ostensibly to inform me that our son was a junkie and that Leo was going to die, she started the conversation as follows: "E isn't around, is she?"

The woman I live with is named Erma, but when Miriam, thrilled by a chance to play up to a crowd, decided to shorten the name to E, Sarah gleefully followed suit. To her mind, a woman who doesn't write, isn't Jewish, doesn't have a father like Leo, and—what's more—is in love with me, can be no more than some sort of clone, a creature human in appearance only.

"C'mon, Sarah, you're not nine years old. Her name is Erma."

"God, you're tiresome. I have the right to say what I want. Apparently she finds my children interesting. Christ! *Interesting!* Tell her to drop dead."

Faced with a brutal day of work and repelled by the idea of wasting my energy on absurd arguments, I simply hung up on her at that point. My sister-in-law Lisa called me back a few hours later, however, and, in a voice strained by sorrow, informed me that: one—Leo had terminal liver cancer; and two—José was apparently shooting drugs, something which had thrown Sarah into a panic but which she herself, knowing her nephew as she did, strongly doubted. I sat there dumbfounded for quite a while, then asked, "Is he in the hospital?"

"José?"

"No, no. Your father."

"You know how he is, Luc. He's decided to stay on his feet to the very end."

"Who's taking care of him?"

"Why, Citrus of course."

I hadn't dared call my father-in-law to ask him how he was doing, fearing that, much as it would not normally have been his style, he might try to talk to me about Sarah. In the car just now, I was thinking only of him but, exasperated by José's implausible drug story—only Sarah could swallow such utter nonsense—I had screamed, "You can die in the gutter for all I care, you little bastard!"

"You'll never change, dad," was all he said in reply.

And now we're walking side by side down one of the paths on the grounds of Echards. I know we're both thinking about Leo. I'd like to say something to comfort my son, but I've never been good at finding words to ease other people's pain. He takes some Kleenex out of his pocket and wipes his eyes. "This really sucks, doesn't it, dad?" he whispers in a choked voice.

And all I can do is hold him a little tighter.

Sarah

Leo's been put in the most comfortable room in the house, the one everyone calls the ghost room because, for generations, children visiting Echards have thought it haunted. As I push the door open, I can hear Miriam's shrill voice. "I'm warning you, grandpa, this one is really disgusting. I'm gonna start, okay? Toto's mother sends him to the store to buy a sausage . . . Is that you, mom?"

My daughter and my sister are holding hands and standing side by side to Leo's right. To his left, the young man who was playing soccer with José is straddling a chair. Paul is standing at one of the windows mopping his brow. He gives me a worried look but calls out in a hearty voice, "Your father has played a joke on us that's in very poor taste."

Someone has unbuttoned the collar of papa's shirt. His complexion suddenly looks very yellow as his lively eyes settle on me. "Billy was right. I did feel like lying down on the ghost bed."

I look at him and mechanically echo, "Billy."

The stranger gives a slight nod in my direction. "That's me, madame. My name is Billy."

He has a slight American accent. Behind his long

wavy lashes, there seems to be a hint of irony glittering in his blue eyes. How old can he be? Somewhere around thirty.

"You should call mom Sarah. Whenever anyone calls her madame, she doesn't like it 'cause it makes her feel old."

"Miriam, you don't have to say everything that comes into your head. What happened to you, papa?"

A heavy silence settles over the room. It's as if they had all come to a tacit agreement not to make any mention of Leo's attack.

"I tripped going up the front steps, treasure."

Those hours spent in the car probably wore him out. Citrus told me in no uncertain terms that a man in my father's condition should be hospitalized in an intensive care unit. But because, like the others, I'll play the game and pretend to forget, for the space of a weekend, that Leo is going to die, I say in a bright voice, "Considering how much you guzzled on the way down here, I'm not exactly shocked."

"My daughters spend their time preaching to me, Billy. They disapprove of my fondness for whiskey."

"Well, we're going to leave you to sleep off your liquor, papa," Lisa proclaims firmly.

She bends down to kiss his cheek and we all start moving toward the door, Paul in the lead. Miriam alone breaks the silence to say, "I'll tell you the one about Toto later, but not in front of mom or Zaza. I'll tell you when it's just the two of us alone."

"Yes, my little darling," Leo replies in a feeble

voice, "you're right—I'm the only one with a proper appreciation for your jokes."

"Rest awhile," Lisa says, breaking in again. "In the meantime, I'll go play on the swings with your grand-daughter."

Once we're out in the hall, however, her confidence disappears. In the very tone of voice she always used when, as a child, something had upset her, she whispers in my ear, "I'm so scared, Sarah."

As soon as they get downstairs, Lisa and Miriam go running arm in arm through the kitchen toward the sandy part of the grounds where the swing-set is kept. José is sitting alone in the drawing room, his face lined with worry, waiting. Luc has disappeared without a trace—he has a pathological fear of everything relating to illness, so it comes as no surprise that he's slipped away. How many times have I heard him muttering that he's had it up to here with the Abners, that band of neurotics? All the same, it's not like Leo got sick on purpose. I put Luc out of my mind and walk over to my son, whose mouth is quivering.

"I didn't have the courage to go upstairs," he admits. "Well, mom?"

"What do you expect? He's tired."

"You aren't going to call a doctor?"

"We have one on the premises," says Paul, pointing, to my surprise, at the young man with the slight American accent. "Our friend took care of Leo in a most calm and efficient manner. Your father claims to have tripped, Sarah, but actually he fell. His legs weren't able to hold him up any longer. Isn't that right, Billy?"

"That's right," Billy replies.

"How do you *know* you're a doctor?" José exclaims. "I thought you couldn't remember a thing ever since you were in that accident."

"It's a little hard to explain, José. You might say I have the feeling that my body wakes up sometimes to tell me how to do things I've learned before."

His casual tone reveals no particular emotion, but as I look at him, I notice that his youthful face has darkened.

"I have an errand to run before the bride-to-be and her parents get here," Paul then says. "Billy has generously offered to go out for fruit juice. Sarah, my dear, could you please drive him?"

Because I want to sound out the young man on Leo's condition anyway, I answer, "Sure. You staying here, José?"

"Yes, I'll keep an eye on grandpa."

"Okay . . . Well, let's get going, Billy."

Outside, Luc is prowling around the Austin. He's wearing the hard expression he's developed during these bad times. I know that when he speaks, his voice will be surly. Does he think a man has to look tough to be taken seriously, or is it that I irritate him? He's so charming when he's relaxed—he would only need to smile at me and I'd fall into his arms.

"This crate of yours looks more disgusting every

time I see it, my poor little Sarah. It's a miracle the thing still runs at all."

"I'm not your poor little Sarah, and instead of worrying about what kind of shape my car is in, you'd do better to try and talk to your kids."

Billy stands there with his arms folded watching the two of us, a dreamy look in his blue eyes.

"Oh right!" shouts Luc, already beside himself. "Know what, Sarah? That'd be a helluva lot easier if you weren't always turning Miriam against me. The girl's impressionable. What an idea, putting her up to calling Erma *E.* Sarah Abner's subtle sense of humor." He turns to Billy. "I'm warning you, sir, beneath that charming exterior lurks a virago."

Billy is all smiles as he shrugs his shoulders and opens the door of the Austin for me. "Please call me Billy," he says to Luc, "and don't worry about me, I know how to take care of myself."

Fed up, I peel out and don't slow down until Luc is no more than a speck in my rearview mirror.

"What's a virago, Sarah?"

"A very nasty woman. I'm really sorry, Billy. These scenes of ours are ridiculous."

"You still love him?"

Caught off-guard by his question, I answer a bit abruptly. "No, no, of course not. For months I felt terrible without knowing why—wounded vanity, I think—and then all of a sudden I realized I was simply missing a familiar object. Listen, I don't want to bore you with my problems, you already have enough worries of your own as it is."

"You aren't boring me, my little virago. I like listening to you."

He runs his fingers lightly along the nape of my neck. I feel myself blush. "Where are we going?" I ask.

He gives a cheerful, innocent laugh. "Let's grab something to drink before we go shopping, okay?"

"Fine."

Billy interrupts me as I try to order an Orangina at the café. "No, a Scotch to improve your spirits, and another one for me because I find you intimidating."

"You find me intimidating? Sure doesn't show."

He's sitting next to me, leaning back against the booth as he watches me silently.

"Billy, why don't you tell me about my father? Are you really a doctor?"

"Yes."

"How do you think he's doing?"

Paul's lodger takes a sip of whiskey, then says, "Poorly. He's running out of strength."

"But he'll be all right for the drive back tomorrow night?"

Billy gazes at me intently with his wide blue eyes that never seem to blink. "Tomorrow, Sarah? I'm just wondering if he's going to make it through the night."

When I begged our old family doctor to tell me the truth about whether Leo had a little more than three months left or a little less, Citrus had seemed pessimistic. But today Billy seems to be saying that it's not a matter of weeks or days, but hours.

"Sarah!"

"What?"

"You're all pale."

"I . . . I didn't know the end was so near. He manages to fool people, you know. I thought he still had a little time left."

As I'm crushing out my cigarette in the ashtray, Billy draws me to him and gently presses his lips against mine. I suddenly feel so cold that I let myself be enveloped by his warmth.

"Your mouth is sweet, virago," he says.

I look at him and suddenly wonder why he lost his memory. "Your accident happened around here?"

"Right near Angers. It was a month ago, around midnight. I must have missed a turn. The rent-a-car I was driving rolled over twice. Paul happened to be passing by. He saw that I looked completely dazed and offered to put me up at his place. I wasn't seriously injured. I just couldn't remember a thing. It's a strange feeling."

"You've really forgotten everything?"

He takes another sip of whiskey before answering.

"Quite a lot. It's all very . . . what's the right word? Nebulous?"

"Hazy?"

"Yes, hazy, thank you. I have found out that my name is William Carver, I'm thirty-two years old, and

I live in Chicago . . . You jumped when I said Chicago.
Do you know the city?"

"A little."

It so happens that in my purse I have an unopened
letter from my mother, Jeanne. The letters come from
the United States once a month. Miriam oftens reads
them before I do. She has no trouble making out
Jeanne's neat handwriting. She'll casually drop the gray
envelope on my desk without comment, but I can tell
she's fascinated.

"Don't you feel like going back home?" I ask.

He shakes his head. "Not before I get what memories I have sorted out. There I'll be, standing in front
of the wife I know I have, and she'll be a complete
stranger. Maybe I wanted to leave her, to abandon my
whole life. I was traveling alone, but I have no idea
what I was doing in Anjou."

Intrigued, I find myself staring at him. One of his
blue eyes has a yellow streak. "Shall we go to the store,
Billy?"

"Yes. I've said too much. Paul loaned me one of
your books."

"Well?"

He smiles. "Well what?"

"Did you like it?"

"Yes and no. You don't quite make it to the bottom of yourself. It's as if something is holding you
back. The fear of saying too much, perhaps."

Leo too has often criticized me for not taking the

plunge. "If you're going to write, treasure, it's not so you can hide, for God's sake!"

But soon I won't have Leo around any more, and I'll have to get used to going on without him. What will I miss the most? Maybe the sound of his voice when he bursts into our apartment unannounced and shouts, "Anybody home?"

José

All I can say is that things aren't exactly going great. Leo's hallucinating in his sleep. When I tiptoed into the ghost room, he said something utterly incomprehensible in Russian. But at that moment, dad was making so much racket out front that *he* was all I could hear.

It upsets me seeing my father so freaked out. The year before he left, he kept getting on my nerves, always yelling over the tiniest things—he was driving everybody at home nuts. Instead of closing a door like a normal person, he'd slam it as hard as he could. I just wanted him to clear out once and for all. But what I didn't get was that underneath it all, he was unhappy. Whenever mom set eyes on him, she'd have this look on her face that went right through him, as if he'd become transparent or wasn't really there. That was what drove him nuts. He'd say, "Shit, Sarah, am I just some sort of cash machine or what? Couldn't you at least pretend to be interested in my job?" But she would just reply distantly in that voice of hers she can change at will, "You know perfectly well that I can't read a blueprint. I get completely lost when I look at all those sketches." I don't mean to pick on my mother or anything, but the old man wasn't exactly wrong either—it wouldn't have been any big deal for her to make a little effort.

Besides, she has a lot of interests. She reads two or three papers a day front to back, not to mention all those paperbacks she tears through, including some she doesn't even like. She goes to the movies all the time. She has the names of all my friends on the tip of her tongue, Miriam's too. And she's up on all the neighborhood gossip because she loves to stand on the front steps and talk with the neighbors about the latest rumors.

But the minute dad starts to discuss his plans, she cups her chin in her hand and looks like she's about to die of boredom. And naturally her pride is wounded now that he's shacked up with E; he calls her his *companion* right in front of us to boot. But at least E—I know this from having eaten with them a lot—at least E loves to listen to him, asks him relevant questions about his work, and occasionally calls him *Luc, darling.* When I hear that, it's all I can do to keep from busting out laughing.

If there's one room I hate at Echards, it's definitely the ghost room. It's this huge, dank room that feels like it's never been touched by the sun, and the windows have these nauseating red-clay-color double curtains that hang all the way down to the floor. When we were little, we'd play in here to scare ourselves, then make a point of screaming as loud as we could to get the room really echoing. They must have put grandpa in here to save time when he had his attack; it's the room closest to the main staircase.

I've never kept watch over a sick person before except for when my sister had peritonitis. I was alone with her one Wednesday. She came into my room looking all waxy, and squawked, "I'm dying, José," then collapsed into my arms. I spent five solid minutes sitting there in a panic before I finally called Citrus. While waiting for the doctor, I heaped ice cubes on her stomach and kept whispering to her that she was going to be okay.

With Leo it's different because he's not going to be okay. His lips move, so I bend toward him and hear him gasp, "Jeanne, my love." Jeanne's my grandmother, the one who left him and her daughters in the lurch to go live in Chicago with a man who apparently made her life hell.

I know a secret about Jeanne that my little sister confessed to me in a moment of weakness. She's tough, that Miriam, and even if she acts like a baby around grown-ups, she's capable of keeping her mouth shut for months, maybe even years, but this thing was just too much for her. One night a good two months ago, she slipped into my room the way she always does when something's not right.

"Will you scoot over so there's room for me in your bed?" she asked in a pitiful voice.

I jammed myself against the wall because her feet are always ice cold, but they grazed me anyway. Then I waited. "Well, Miriam?"

She whispered something I couldn't make out.

"What is it? Speak up!"

"Mom can't hear. Listen, José, there's this lady who comes to see me at school."

"Who?"

She sighed heavily. "Wait."

"That's really dangerous, Miriam. You know you shouldn't talk to anyone, I mean, not to anyone you don't know."

"It's not just anyone."

"No? Well, come on then, spit it out. How old is this lady?"

"She's halfway old, José. The other times she asked me not to say anything and just took me out for a soda. But today she was wearing dark glasses 'cause she'd been crying. Her eyes were all red behind the glasses. She told me she'd really like to see you too."

I kept wracking my brain, and still I couldn't figure out for the life of me who this halfway-old lady could be. But you have to take it easy with my sister. Otherwise she clams up completely. "So why does she want to see us so much?" I asked.

Miriam whispered into my ear, "Because she doesn't know her grandchildren. Get it?"

At that moment I thought of Ludo and the time he told me, "I love spending time with your family. The atmosphere's completely crazy—it's like being in another country." Ludo would have been in seventh heaven: a grandmother we've never seen sends us letters from Chicago every month, and meanwhile she's showing up at Miriam's school.

"Yes, I get it," I said to my sister. "It's Jeanne, Leo's wife. Has she been picking you up at school for a long time?"

"Since Christmas."

"And what about the letters, the ones from America? Who's been sending them if she's here?"

"I dunno," Miriam answered drowsily. "I didn't ask her. You gonna come see her?"

"Maybe. Now get back to bed."

Leo stirs in his sleep. "Jeanne, my love," he murmurs. I look at him carefully, but his eyes stay closed. Should I tell him I've seen the woman he's dreaming about?

I staked out Miriam's school from behind one of the billboards belonging to a nearby carpet store and kept staring at the little group of parents, trying to figure out which one was my unknown grandmother. But I was looking for a little old lady when in fact Miriam ended up running into the arms of a tall, slender woman. As she turned, I caught a glimpse not only of her tired, lined face, but also of her eyes—they were as big as mom's. I have a real aversion to scenes—I've been through my share with the parents where first they're arguing, then they're shouting, and finally they're making up right there in the middle of the street or in the car—so I didn't jump out from behind the billboard and say "Here I am" to Jeanne. Instead, I watched them turn onto Keller, and by the time they disappeared from view, I'd already made up my mind.

Maybe it was out of solidarity with my aunt Lisa, who hates Jeanne with all her might, but for whatever reason, I would not go up to this woman who had abandoned her daughters. I mean, it's too easy just to show up one fine day as if nothing has happened. Besides, at that point I was busy playing drug addict, and then grandpa got sick, so I forgot all about Jeanne when my sister didn't mention her again. The only thing I did was ask Ludo what he would do if he were in my shoes, and all he said was, "Pal, the things that go on in your family never cease to amaze me. At least it's never dull at your house. All the same, I'd still say she must have had some good reason for coming."

For the third time, Leo clearly utters the phrase, "Jeanne, my love." Leo—*he's* the good reason. Someone must have told her about his condition. Probably Citrus, who was a good friend of hers before she left for Chicago. We've only known for three weeks, but Citrus must have been aware of the situation for a long time.

I hear the door open behind me. Dad whispers, "How's he doing?"

"Not great," I answer. "He's delirious."

"You don't mind if I stay here with you for a little while?"

"No, no, dad, of course not."

Reassured, he sits down on the chair at the foot of

the bed where Billy was sitting and gazes fondly at Leo. Occasionally my dad forgets to play the hard-boiled tough guy, the one you can't put anything over on, and at those moments he radiates this incredible warmth. When I was little, he'd come into my room almost every night to watch me sleep. Sensing his presence, I'd open my eyes drowsily and he'd flash a smile at me—the nice one that lights up his whole face. Then he'd put two fingers on my forehead and murmur, "Sweet dreams, José." Another time I saw him crying without making a sound. I asked him, "What's wrong, dad?" and he murmured, "I don't know how to put it into words—they always fail me. I hope you won't grow up to be like me."

I wonder if mom suspects that underneath it all my father is a soft-hearted sentimentalist. She probably hasn't been forgiving enough with him. See, she's the tough guy in the family, even if not that many people know it. Beneath that absentminded, hesitant exterior lurks this determination to have her way at all costs. I think dad has wasted a lot of energy trying to prove he's stronger than she is. And if there's one thing she can't stand, it's anyone questioning her decisions, which is exactly what dad used to do all the time, probably because he was afraid that if he didn't, he'd look weak and ridiculous.

Leo's breathing seems strange to me. It's as if he were trying to catch his breath. I had always imagined that my grandfather was indestructible. This is the first time I've ever seen him sick or even worn out. Obviously he used to down phenomenal amounts of whiskey, but all the same he always had a healthy complexion and that piercing gaze that made such an impression on Miriam when she was little.

"You think he's going to pull through?" I whisper.

My father frowns. He hesitates before answering softly. "I'd like to be able to put your mind at ease, José, but I think Leo is really sick. Tell yourself that you were fortunate enough to know a kind of man you don't meet very often—a genuinely decent one."

I look at him.

He lowers his eyes and adds in a whisper, "I really admire your mother, you know. I'm sorry that . . . well, that . . . ."

At that point his voice breaks.

"Dad," I say without thinking, "why don't you try moving back home?"

He shrugs his shoulders. "Drop it, José," he replies in that surly tone I hate. "I'd just be in the way."

But I stay on the offensive—you don't get many chances like this with dad.

"Do you love Erma?"

"That's none of your business," he hisses.

We both fall silent there next to the bed. I'm keeping an eye on Leo's breathing but thinking about my father. Dad puts on an act in public. In fact, it drives mom nuts the way, as she puts it, he breaks out his charm around people who don't count, people he'll never see again, whereas he's standoffish and tight-lipped with her. But I'm quite sure that underneath it all, he's scared to death of being rejected.

Outside, beyond this gloomy room's windows, I can hear Miriam squealing. As she bursts out laughing, Leo opens his eyes and raises his head. "Is that you, children? I'm glad to see you, Luc, you look well."

Dad starts to say something, but grandpa has already fallen back to sleep.

"What does he say when he's delirious, José?"

Not knowing what to say, I hem and haw for a moment. Out of some kind of loyalty to Leo, I answer, "Oh, nothing in particular."

"That's funny. As I was walking in the door, he was saying 'Jeanne, my love.' "

I had forgotten that my father's step is so light you can barely hear it. He's given me the creeps many times by suddenly materializing behind me when I least expected it.

"Yeah," I say, "could be."

Dad looks at me askance. "Listen, Joe"—he often calls me Joe in private—"didn't you ever want to meet your grandmother?"

I shrug my shoulders. "Not really."

"Because if you wanted to, it could be arranged."

I make up my mind to play dumb and not show any outward surprise. But my old man plows straight ahead, unfazed, and says, "Jeanne's in Paris, you know. Citrus wrote her that Leo wasn't doing well, so she flew in from Chicago. She called me last week, can you imagine? I had lunch with her day before yesterday. I think she'd really like to see her grandchildren."

I can just imagine him and Jeanne together, the two Abner clan rejects airing their grievances. Leo's personality was too much for Jeanne, same with mom—I mean for dad—so dad and Jeanne both cut out. Easy enough to complain after the fact. Without looking up, I grumble, "She sure took her time about making up her mind."

My father abruptly jumps to his feet. "You're heartless, Joe, just like your mother. Pretending to be a junkie, what a crock!"

To my surprise, the moment Dad leaves the ghost room, Leo opens his eyes. Without a hint of drowsiness, he says in a perfectly normal voice, "Now that we're alone, we're going to have a serious chat. It's time for me to tell you about the past, José. Yes, it's definitely time."

Luc

Perhaps José has forgotten that he used to call me mama when he was little. When I brought him and Sarah home from the hospital after he was born, Sarah handed me this squeaking bundle and told me, "I didn't have a mother, so I won't know how to take proper care of him. You'll show me how it's done, won't you, Luc?"

I changed José's diapers, bathed him, fed him. I was even the one who got up every night at feeding time to put him in Sarah's arms, then watched her fall asleep while breast-feeding her own son. No doubt I was different then. My goal wasn't to become a man with a successful career, I just wanted to be happy. I felt an unlimited admiration for Sarah, whose talents, I sensed, were more exceptional than my own. She was the one who declared one fine day that I wasn't ambitious enough, or was it aggressive enough—I no longer remember just what word it was she used—and that it was high time I got on with my life rather than wasting my talents on the same old routine.

Up until then, I had worked as an architect for other people and been perfectly content to do so. In spite of Leo's warning—he felt that I was no businessman—she talked me into striking out on my own. Spurred by the extraordinary interest she seemed to be showing in my career, I borrowed money right and left to start up my own firm. I found a partner and began slaving away sixteen hours a day.

By the time Miriam was born, I no longer had a minute to myself. I was never *mama* to Miriam. No, to her I was the guy who came home late at night after she had already gone to sleep and withdrawn into her little girl world. Sarah, of course, forgot that if I was working so hard to make a name for myself, it was in large measure on account of her constant urgings, and began accusing me of having changed. Encourage her as I might to accompany me to the gallery openings and dinner parties to which I was frequently invited, she would usually decline, her excuse being that she couldn't let herself squander the least bit of time. In any event, whenever her imagination flagged or her wit dried up, it was my fault. The incredible commotion collectively generated by the kids, Leo, Lisa, friends who had stopped by for a drink, and so on . . . anyway, all that noise didn't disturb her in the slightest, whereas my least little act would bring a sullen look of disapproval to her face.

In spite of my countless faults, I still remained her first reader—even if I was no longer, strictly speaking, her partner, since we did everything else separately. Much as I remained curious to find out what she had produced, I dreaded those sessions, and with good reason. I'd come home from the office or a job site exhausted and know just by looking at the way she was clutching a sheaf of pages to her breast that the moment of reading was upon us.

With Sarah urging me on, I'd wolf down my dinner. Then, when she handed me her latest creation, I had to express wild enthusiasm before seeing even the first line. Nor would she let me read in peace. Instead, she would perch herself across from me on the armrest of one of the leather easy chairs and, arms folded, search my face for the slightest hint of a reaction, chain-smoking all the while. If I had the misfortune to emit even the beginnings of a sigh, she'd mutter in a choked voice, "Fine, put it down. I understand. I'm going to chuck the whole thing out the window and me with it," or something equally inane. If, on the other hand, I looked moved or amused, she'd descend on me like a hurricane to see what passage had provoked the reaction. Without showing the slightest shame in interrupting me during my ordeal (in spite of the adulation I felt for her, an ordeal it was—I defy anyone to manage to stay calm under such dreadful conditions), she would exclaim, "Oh yes, I like that bit too." Then she'd immediately reveal what was about to happen on the next page. When she finally calmed down again, we'd each resume our previous positions and I would continue reading, sometimes until the wee hours of the morning, doing my best to keep my eyes open lest I touch off another outburst by looking fatigued.

Then came that terrible moment when she would ask for my opinion. If it was favorable, she'd suspect me of being indulgent out of cowardice, and if it wasn't, she'd accuse me of not understanding anything; indeed, of no longer loving her. For above all, Sarah remains a sensitive, thin-skinned, excessive, paranoid creature—in short, a writer. Some mornings my current companion, Erma, wakes me by bringing me coffee in bed. Occasionally, as she's handing me the cup, I think in my half-waking state that it's Sarah's infamous manuscript pages again coming my way.

As I'm leaving the room where they've put Leo—the one called the ghost room that scared me to death when I would play in it as a child—I think again of those Abners. I know why I agreed to see Jeanne, Leo's wife. Much as I'm loath to admit it, I feel a sort of nostalgia for what used to aggravate me so much when I lived with Sarah. The moment I'd open the door, I'd feel as if I'd run headfirst into a cyclone. Muddled conversations, improbable projects, Jewish jokes when Leo was around—it all came together and formed a continuous vibration. Even their occasional silences struck me as frantic, as if electrically charged. I would be greeted offhandedly, and no one would ever deign to ask me how *my* day had gone.

After having been shunted to one side by the Abner clan like some piece of broken-down furniture, I would serve myself a whiskey, then settle into a corner with my newspaper and do my best to block out all the commotion. Just as I would be starting to feel relaxed, Sarah would plant herself in front of me and invariably exclaim in her coldest voice, "Would it be too much for you to say hello and ask me if my work went well today?" At that point Miriam would suddenly turn up as well and, using the same reproachful tone as her mother, chime in, "And what about me, daddy? Don't you want to know what I did at school today? Oh, by the way, you got five francs?" A cash dispenser, that's what I was to them. As for architecture, they really couldn't have cared less. Those last few weeks, when I felt like lining them all up and shooting them, I'd slam out of the apartment and run over to my best friend Maxime's place.

And yet, the irritating chaos that prevailed in our home radiated a harmony that I can only explain by likening it to a kind of love. Did they love me? No doubt they did, in their own way. Unfortunately, I wasn't exotic enough or marginal enough or Jewish enough to be part of the clan. My wife and children would criticize me over the slightest details. For example, I often wear ties to work, something which moved them to fits of laughter in the morning. "You look like one of those old guys in the movies, daddy," Miriam would roar between gulps of hot chocolate. Then Sarah would add: "Or like a banker." Now Sarah, when she isn't wearing jeans, decks herself out in a way which may well flatter her angular grace but which I would charitably describe as eccentric. No matter how carefully I explained that I couldn't dress like a punk rocker or a metal head when taking a client to lunch, she would merely shrug her shoulders disdainfully. Maybe I just wasn't her type. Maybe she would have preferred some well-tanned hunk like this Billy who seems to turn up every time you turn around this weekend. In any event, on those particular mornings she would proclaim, before the children as her witnesses, that the more old-fashioned I looked, the less business I would bring in. Because for her, wearing a tie is old-fashioned—save when Leo wears one.

Poor Leo. When I was in the ghost room, I felt more upset than I did beside my own father's death bed. But I refuse to continue thinking in this vein. It's too late. The Abner page of my life has been turned and I no longer have to answer to the woman I loved beyond all reasonable limits.

Feeling vaguely bitter, I idly pace the drawing room floor. Erma made me promise to call her. She senses that I don't belong to her one hundred percent, that some inexplicable quirk prevents me from loving her the way I loved Sarah—Sarah's smell, Sarah's skin, Sarah's step, Sarah's laugh. She knows it, so she has deftly snared me in her net, and I'm caught. I needed to be admired, but now I'm suffocating. I dial her number.

"Hello," she says, answering at the first ring. "Is that you, sweetie?"

Erma has her points. She's affectionate, calm, and organized, and she actually says hello when I come home to her place at night, but *sweetie* leaves me cold. "Yes, it's Luc," I say in an unavoidably cool tone.

Unruffled, she goes on. "You're holding up? Things aren't too bad?"

"I'm doing all right."

"I suppose your wife's putting you through hell?"

In spite of everything, I hate it when anyone else criticizes Sarah.

"No, no, not at all," I reply, then add hastily, "I'm calling you as promised, but I can't talk for long. There's quite a throng pressing in behind me."

"Of course, sweetie, I understand."

There she goes again. At the next *sweetie*, I'm settling this matter once and for all.

"Who are you talking to on the phone, dad?" Miriam asks insistently from behind me.

I put my hand over the mouthpiece and whisper, "Nobody."

"You're losing your marbles! You can't be talking to nobody! Hey, I'll bet it's E."

I flash a smile in spite of myself. Maybe if I called Erma E too, I'd be spared that awful *sweetie* of hers. "Okay, you win. Now please get out of here, darling."

But my daughter continues to stand there next to me waiting for God knows what. All I can do now is whisper into the phone, "I'm going to hang up now. Talk to you tomorrow."

Two pairs of eyes are looking me over intently: Lisa's green ones and Miriam's rather more amber-colored pair.

"Can I get you a gin and tonic, Luc?" asks my sister-in-law.

Stifling a sigh, I nod. She hasn't changed since the time I had that fling with her. Yes, I screwed my wife's little sister, night and day, for one torrid week during the month of August a few years back. She and I both found ourselves alone in Paris, she because she had decided to spend the entire summer at her job with the National Center for Scientific Research, I because I was rushing to meet a deadline for a national competition. She phoned me one night at the office to beg a favor.

"I'd be happy to do you any favor you like. Just name it."

"Oh, I've been incredibly naïve. Sarah warned me. I should have listened to her."

The Abner sisters have little in common in terms of either appearance or personality, but one trait they do share is being utterly incapable of getting straight to the point. Knowing this, I waited patiently.

"Luc, are you still there?"

"Yes, yes."

"You remember Jerry?"

"Jerry's the archery champ? The one you took in after they let him out of the nuthouse?"

"No," she replied, "Jerry isn't a champ at anything, but I'd certainly love to have him committed. Tonight he started beating me because he'd been drinking. Now he's barricaded himself inside my bedroom and refuses to leave."

In spite of the sympathy I felt for Lisa, I couldn't help rolling my eyes.

"And you want me to come drive him away?"

There was a momentary pause, then the answer. "Yes, precisely."

After succeeding in kicking Jerry out, I took Lisa

to dinner. I don't know why exactly, but somehow her black eye really turned me on. As we were finishing our meal, she fired a stern look my way and said, "Listen, Luc, it wouldn't be sensible."

She was absolutely right, of course. Sarah would have been quite capable of killing both of us. But I had insisted on having one last drink at her place, and without knocking her around the way Jerry had, I got her undressed in record time. Much as I felt sick with guilt, for the next six days I would rush over to Lisa's place any time I had a spare minute. At the end of the week, we said goodbye, each of us knowing that it was over. I met up with Sarah and the kids, who had been vacationing on the coast, and when we got back, Lisa was as friendly and relaxed as if nothing had happened.

At the moment, she's handing me my gin and tonic. "It was nice of you to come," she says. Then, taking advantage of the fact that Miriam has gone upstairs to see if Leo has awakened, she adds, "Are you happy, at least?"

A typically Abnerian question. "Do you really expect an answer?" I reply a bit curtly.

She narrows those cat eyes of hers and stares at me. "Why don't you try talking to Sarah a little? She'll never admit it, but she misses you, you know."

I look down to avoid her gaze. "Could be, but I've been through too much."

I can't bring myself to admit that her sister's self-centeredness has pushed me over the edge . . . Am I happy? No, of course not. I have my job, Erma, a few buddies, but without Sarah and the children, I feel as if a part of myself has been amputated. If I start dwelling on it, start dissecting my past, I can see that everything's fouled up. So I'm throwing in the towel.

Sarah

Fact is, I don't know exactly why I became a writer. A series of chance events, I guess. I could have been something more honorable and serious, like a lawyer—except that knowing myself as I do, I'm sure I would have started giggling right in the middle of a summation. Luc often used to criticize me for not having any respect for this, that, or the other. If I make light of everything, it's no doubt because mockery protects me from life's rough spots. When I lose my sense of humor, my outlook quickly turns black and I have only one desire: to throw myself out the window or light myself on fire—something of that nature. As early on as kindergarten, I would hide my shyness by making everybody laugh.

To get back to literature, a rather grand word . . . I first started writing because of Lisa. As I was to do later with my own children, I got into the habit of telling her a story every night. "A story from your head," she would invariably insist. I'd start out traditionally enough with fairies and dragons, but as soon as something I said made her chuckle, I'd be off and running. It was amazing. All I had to do was hear her roaring with laughter—Lisa has the most contagious laugh I know—and my imagination would take flight. Leo would occasionally come sit in my room for those sessions, and one day it was he who advised me to transcribe the bedtime stories I improvised for my sister. In a closet somewhere I still have several notebooks covered with my meticulous schoolgirl script. Lisa, however, grew tired of my demented witches, and I did not write anything at all for many years.

One June day at the time I was half-heartedly bringing my literary studies to a close, a well-known stand-up comedian who had gone to school with Citrus came for dinner at our place on rue La Bruyère. During the course of the meal, he told us of his troubles, a desolate look on his face. It had been quite some time since he'd had any inspiration whatsoever. "Making an audience laugh is hell," he told us, and to top it all off, the young man who'd been writing some of his material had had the bad taste to commit suicide.

"I know someone who could help you out," exclaimed Lisa. While I looked daggers at her, our dinner guest inquired as to this person's identity. "It's Sarah," my sister replied without missing a beat. "She can really be funny when she puts her mind to it."

The comedian turned to me. I was painfully shy around strangers as a rule, and this time had been no exception—I hadn't unclenched my jaws all night. "Things have gotten so bad, I'd be a fool not to give it a shot," he said. "You don't look very funny, my girl, but I'm in a position to know how little that means. Let's give it a try. I noticed the way you were watching me during dinner. You seem to know how to use the eyes the good Lord gave you. So write me two pages about people you find amusing. That is, unless you have any objections, Monsieur Abner."

Leo, who didn't weigh himself down with prejudices, replied, "Why, none at all."

Anyway, the comedian liked my two pages, and I became his ghostwriter. A year later, I finished my first novel, a melodrama to provide me with a change of pace after all those jokes I had to whip up on demand for my employer. I received a certain degree of critical acclaim, something that dumbfounded my nearest and dearest, and even a few fan letters from readers who said my writing had moved them to tears. That response pleased me, for up until then, at home and in school, I had only been one to elicit laughter.

When I met Luc at Echards, I was twenty-four years old and already a novelist. The thing I liked most about him was his incredible sweetness. Much as he displayed a great deal of social grace in public, I could see through to his vulnerable, almost wounded, core. We came from completely different, indeed opposite, backgrounds. Our tribe fascinated him. Leo has always mixed together his plethora of friends without the least hesitation. Jewish craftsmen and merchants, some of whom spoke practically nothing but Yiddish, would rub elbows with eminent university professors at our place on rue La Bruyère. My own friends—artists and actors for the most part—were added to that circle, along with Lisa's more serious ones, who were mathematicians and physicists like herself. Thus, our house was always filled with a tumultuous warmth. I was so thoroughly imbued with those sounds which, in a certain sense, soothed me as a child that now, unlike many writers, I cannot stand to work surrounded by silence. I need excitement, music, screaming children.

Anyway, Luc was at once taken aback and charmed by the unconventional atmosphere generated by what he quickly dubbed *the Abner clan*. As for me, I was extremely impressed by the effortless good manners that characterized Luc's family. Whereas we in our family had the annoying habit of recapping the day's events by shouting across the apartment at the top of our lungs, at the home of The Royals, as my sister and I took to calling them, one expressed oneself in a calm and dignified manner.

I was to discover later, by way of Luc's silences, that in his family the most important things never got said. Luc's feeling of discomfort with himself no doubt came from the excessive reticence that was the rule among the Pottiers. Since he didn't know how to put his feelings into words, he would hide them to the point of becoming estranged from his own emotions. No, Luc is one person I've never understood. At first I made a sincere, if highly awkward, effort to wrest from him what lurked in the depths of his heart or guts or whatever it is that holds the truth about a person, and then one day, more or less at the time Miriam was born, I gave up. Maybe I didn't love him enough to keep trying.

"What are you thinking about, my virago?"

I abruptly return to the present—the cloudy March sky, the little stream, the crunching sound my old car's tires make on the gravel driveway . . .

"Nothing," I reply, then add, "So I'm to be your virago from now on?"

"Yes, that certainly sounds cooler than Sarah."

I park right near the kitchen door. Luc is apparently calmer than he was when we left. He helps Billy unload the drinks we bought at the store. Determined to act friendly so as not to spoil the weekend completely, I send a smile my husband's way, but he just eyes me suspiciously. Ever since he's been living with Erma, a meticulous woman whose every gesture would seem to be meticulously rehearsed, he imagines that I calculate everything too. He's forgotten that he used to criticize me for the very way in which, in his opinion, I was raising the children by intuition and conducting my career irrationally. In spite of his sullen look, I force myself to say, "How are things going, Luc?"

"You mean with Leo?"

"No, with you."

"With me? Same as ever. I haven't suddenly turned into a comedian or a wordsmith. I'm putting in a lot of time at the office, if that could possibly interest you."

After suddenly emerging from God knows where, Miriam is hanging from my arm. "Mommy, daddy called E."

I prudently correct her. "Erma, darling. Daddy has the right to phone anyone he likes. And besides, no one asked you to go blabbing everything you know."

"That's not true," shouts my daughter. "Every time we see E, you always ask us to tell you exactly what she was wearing and . . ."

I stick a hand over Miriam's mouth, but to my surprise, Luc has not gotten angry. He's gazing at both of us with a vaguely melancholy look. "It was wrong of me to get so upset just now," he says.

"Don't worry about it," I reply, a lump in my throat, then fall silent. His brutality petrifies me, but this unexpected patience moves me to the point of tears. For once I'm the one who looks away first. I should talk to him about his work, ask him some relevant questions about it. But then, what do I remember about the activities that occupy his days? Between the cities, blueprints, renovations, and reconstructions, I used to get lost as if trapped in some complicated maze, so I wouldn't ask anything—out of a fear of appearing stupid during the first few years, then out of simple laziness at the end. He has every right to complain; I've been the most negligent of wives. I finally succeed in reining in my emotions and ask in a calm voice, "How's your work going?"

Someone told me he had just won a competition. A whole city to restore, or something like that. I should congratulate him, but no polite phrase comes to mind. The comedian, who has left the stage and is now retired, maintained that he had never seen anyone more pathetic than I when it came to dispensing compliments. Like all professional comedians, he himself laughed rarely, indeed hardly at all. But my stone-faced expression when he would come off stage and ask, "So, was I good?" was one of the few things that could break him up. Luc, on the other hand, derives no amusement from my inability to gush over his various projects. He bitterly rebuked me one day, saying, "You take such great pride in being warm and open, but you're completely indifferent to me. You barely even know I exist."

It's not that I'm indifferent, just that I'm shy and clumsy. Truth is, I have about as much tact as an elephant. And because I have a reputation for being funny all the time, I prefer keeping quiet to shouting *bravo* with an involuntary tremor that, more often than not, brings only confusion.

"So now you're interested in my job?" marvels Luc. "That's a new one."

Miriam is watching us anxiously. Our quarrels used to terrify her. But unlike José, who'd prudently beat a retreat into his bedroom, she'd go right to the front lines in an attempt to referee her parents' conflicts.

"Maybe I've changed."

"You, Sarah? I'd be shocked. You've never exactly had a passion for architecture. Apart from your precious writing, you don't give a damn about anything."

Leaning back against the Austin, he lights a Camel straight. Billy has disappeared into the house; Paul isn't back yet; Lisa is taking a walk; and José's sitting with his grandfather. We'd be alone if our daughter, firmly planted between us on legs showing no signs of budging, weren't vigilantly observing us. Forgetting my good intentions, I shoot back, "And what about you? Did you ever listen to me when I'd tell you about my day? You're a fine one to talk. The minute you got home, you'd bury yourself in the newspaper. I'd try to ask you questions about your projects, and you'd just grumble that I didn't understand a thing about them."

"You definitely haven't changed," replies Luc.

"Mommy, daddy," says Miriam imploringly, "stop fighting."

Surprised and vaguely ashamed, we look at each other. As I affectionately ruffle my daughter's hair, I make out my sister's silhouette near the stream at the far edge of the front lawn. Did I say anything after that week-long affair of theirs a few years back? Naturally neither one of them let anything slip, and I didn't ask any questions. Concealing my rage and jealousy, I made a conscious effort to play the absentminded artist. Had my rival been anyone other than Lisa, I would have reacted differently.

But I've always protected my little sister, especially since that terrible night when she swallowed half a bottle of plant fertilizer. I was coming home from the Olympia Theatre, where my employer had just made a triumphant return to the stage. At that time Leo was keeping company with a woman his own age and would frequently end up spending the night with her.

Lisa had just had her heart broken for the first time, but in spite of my urgings, she stubbornly refused to come with me to the music hall. While Leo and I were away, she stayed home alone with a quiche Lorraine and a mystery novel she was leafing through glumly. When I got back and saw the light on in the large bedroom we shared, I shouted, "You really missed something, Zaza. I laughed out loud at my own jokes, and so did the audience. Zaza, where are you? You asleep?"

Walking on tiptoe so as not to wake her, I went up to the bedroom door and carefully pushed it open. There, sprawled on her back between our two beds, arms draped over her chest and the bottle of fertilizer lying near her, was Lisa, still breathing. A thin, raspy sound seemed to be tearing her lungs. I threw myself down next to her, probably with the intention of infusing her with a little of my warmth.

"Lisa, don't die," I begged her. "Oh, my little Lisa."

I finally got a grip on myself and called an ambulance. Then I phoned our brave friend Citrus, who declared, "She'll pull through—don't be so worried," before clasping me very tightly to his chest.

"You poor girls," he sighed at the local hospital, where he had insisted on staying with me while I waited for Lisa. "It's a painful ordeal growing up without a mother's affection. Leo's done what he could, but Jeanne never should have left. And to think she felt she was acting in your best interest. I'll never forget the day she came to tell me that she was leaving. She figured she wouldn't know how to raise you kids in any normal way, and I couldn't figure out how to convince her to stay. What I needed to do was reassure her. She had so little confidence in herself that she was afraid of hurting you two by staying. What nonsense!"

"What should I do for Lisa, Dr. Citrus?" I asked.

"Exactly what you always do—love her very much."

As day was breaking and my sister was finally out of danger, I saw Leo really sobbing for the first time . . .

And now Lisa is walking across the lawn toward us. Her eyes are opened wide and sparkling with delight. "The bride-to-be is here," she informs us. "The festivities are about to begin."

I look Luc straight in the eye and see the face of the young man I fell in love with here at the wedding of some long forgotten little cousin. But he has turned to Lisa and already cannot see me.

José

My grandfather has gotten his sly smile back. He's propped himself up against the headboard of the bed. His gaze locks onto mine.

"You're a fine boy," he says. "Naming you Jeremiah would have been a crime. You really love me, right?"

I can't hold back my tears and have to make a concerted effort not to start bawling before I can answer. Even so my voice catches in the back of my throat. " 'Course, Leo. I got butterflies in my stomach watching you sleep."

"Was I talking?"

Embarrassed, I look away. "Yeah, a little."

But, to my relief, he doesn't ask what he said. And now he's beckoning to me. "Come closer, José. I want to be able to see you clearly. You have the most candid face I've ever seen. I think when you reach adulthood, your finest quality will be tolerance."

First he has me on the verge of tears; then he makes me blush. What can I say? It's true that Leo's the person I love most in this world after mom. I'm sitting next to him and can feel his warmth surrounding me.

For a few minutes, we both remain silent. Then I say, "You wanted to tell me about the past, grandpa."

"Ah yes," he goes, "that's right. Where do you want me to begin?"

I shrug my shoulders. "I don't know, that's up to you."

He reaches reflexively for his ever-present hip flask. "They're going to take everything," he sighs.

Leo never launches into one of his beloved anecdotes without first wetting his whistle. He looks at me imploringly, but I stand firm. "You're going to do without your liquor for once, Leo," I say. "Mom would bawl us both out, and you know her—when she gets mad, it's no picnic."

He nods in agreement. "Oh, yes, I certainly do know her. Even when she was little, she'd throw such incredible tantrums that the walls of our apartment would shake. But you know, she liked it too when I'd tell her about my memories. 'I want to know how it was in the old days,' she'd say. Lisa, on the other hand, would refuse to listen. Those two little girls were inseparable, but so completely different from one another."

His lively eyes grow hazy as soon as he starts conjuring up Mom and Lisa's childhood. Personally, I think he regrets that they didn't stay little forever, sitting hand in hand and staring wide-eyed, the way they are captured in the old photograph that rules his nightstand.

"I killed my mother in childbirth, something for

which my father never forgave me. I spent years trying in every conceivable way to make him love me, but to no avail."

"Leo," I break in, "that's stuff you've already told me."

"Mmmm, so I have. You want to know how I met Jeanne and under what circumstances she left. Your mother was always asking me those same questions too: 'Why, why, why did she go and leave the three of us like that?' " Chin in hands, he gathers his thoughts.

"Yes, why?" I ask.

He looks at me but doesn't see me. Behind me I hear a creaking sound. I don't turn around, however, because in this room the floorboards creak and those awful clay-red drapes rustle in the breeze coming through the windows. My father is always telling me how when he was a kid, he'd get all frightened playing hide-and-seek with his cousins in here because he'd think he felt the ghost breathing down his neck.

"Grandpa, are you falling asleep?" I whisper.

"No, José," he goes in a voice so soft I have to bend forward to hear it. "I've slept enough. Tell me something. Who's the most beautiful woman you've ever seen?"

Without taking the time to reflect, I open my mouth and the words spill out. "My mom," I hear myself say, then, dying of embarrassment, I flush beet red.

But I don't sense any hint of irony in Leo's reaction. On the contrary, he nods with a look of tender understanding. "Well for me," he whispers, "the most beautiful woman was Jeanne. But, of course, your mother is the spitting image of her."

"Really?" I say in an offhand tone, since I'm not supposed to know what Jeanne looks like.

Grandpa folds his arms, his eyes half closed and, forgetting that his whiskey's missing, launches into his story. "It was that damned Citrus who introduced me to her, in 1938. At that time everyone who was flee-ing the Nazis or Stalin's purges would find their way to his place. Sometimes he'd end up housing as many as twenty people in his little student apartment. One morning he phoned me and simply said, 'By the way, I've got a new lodger. She's fresh off the boat from Kovno, your hometown. The girl's a real looker, but she hasn't opened her mouth since she got here two days ago. I need you, Leo. You've gotta come cheer her up.' When he added that her name was Jeanne, I was taken aback. You see, kid, where I'm from, people don't have that name. In Lithuania, the women were named Lisa like your great-grandmother, or Paula, or Ida, and so on. 'Jeanne?' I repeated. 'You sure?' 'Apparently her mother's French,' he re-plied, then added, 'Hurry up, I'm waiting.' You re-member, José, how after my military service I was working as a waiter at a café right in the heart of the Latin Quarter. I'd had enough of refugees, so it was with no great enthusiasm that I trudged over there. 'A real looker,' I muttered to myself as I walked, 'and just what else?' "

All of a sudden, Leo stops talking and pricks up his ears.

"What is it, grandpa?" I ask.

"I thought I heard a sigh, kid."

"Oh, it's just the ghost," I reply. "Go on. He won't eat you. So what was she like, this Jeanne?"

His eyes mist over. "The face of an angel. The most perfect features I've ever seen. I married her a month later. And yet, I sensed from the first that she wasn't really in love with me. I made her laugh, I was constantly surprising her, she probably admired me—but she didn't love me. When I came back from the camps, she had met someone else—a boy of eighteen who liked to play the part of the great resistance fighter. Sarah was born, and for a long time I held out hope that she'd forget her little schoolboy. She kept seeing him on the sly and I closed my eyes to it. And then along came Lisa."

He breaks off. Cautiously, I whisper, "What about Lisa?"

My heart is racing in my chest, racing because I've guessed what it is that grandpa doesn't dare say.

"I've never known if she was really my daughter."

A piercing cry suddenly rings out in the ghost room. I don't need to turn around to know who's there behind us, hidden by the half-open door.

"What are you doing here, my little darling?" whispers Leo. "Are you playing ghost?"

"There's no such thing as ghosts," Miriam moans.

"Me neither, grandpa," she whimpers. "I'm not my daddy's real daughter either. Otherwise he wouldn't have left."

Her face streaked with tears, she throws herself on Leo's bed. "And if you go and die, who'm I going to have to love me? The minute I open my mouth at home, I get yelled at. Mom likes José better. She's always saying 'my José this and my José that,' blah, blah, blah. I don't count for beans."

Leo ruffles her hair before hugging her to his chest. "Have you been listening to us for a long time, pussycat?" he asks her gently.

"For a very long time."

While I watch my little sister trembling despondently in Leo's arms, I'm thinking to myself that of the two of us, she's the one who's caught the brunt of things. For six months, nobody's taken the trouble to explain to her that in spite of all the carryings-on at home, we still love her as much as ever. And as for me, her older brother, I should have been comforting her instead of screwing around with this junkie stuff.

"So Zaza isn't your real daughter?" she whispers.

Looking over Miriam's head, our grandfather gives me a piercing look, then turns to her and says, "Why, of course she's my daughter . . . Look at me. How old are you?"

Caught by surprise, she immediately stops crying before answering. "Oh, grandpa! Have you lost your mind? You know perfectly well that I'm nine. You even gave me a skateboard for my birthday, and when we tried it out in the street, I ran right over you and you fell on your bottom. And you told me . . ."

"Yes." Leo smiles. "I moaned that the memory of your ninth birthday was going to be forever imprinted on my rear end. Let's get back to what I wanted to explain to you. You're not such a little girl any more."

She looks pensively at each of us in turn. "No." I detect a trace of mom's singsong way of talking in her voice.

"Well, you heard something you shouldn't have," continues our grandfather. "That may be just as well. In life, things don't happen the way they do in books. People have this infuriating habit of getting things all muddled. You think you're fine, that nothing's ever going to change, then suddenly one of the people around you goes and does something unexpected. And then, of course, everything you're used to gets turned upside down and you're completely lost. Listen . . ."

Miriam squirms impatiently. "Say whatever you want, grandpa, but the truth is that daddy doesn't love me any more. I'm sure I'm not his real daughter."

Leo sighs helplessly. When he's on the wagon, his powers of persuasion aren't what they usually are.

I break in to help him. "Miriam, you aren't the milkman's daughter, you know."

"What milkman? I want mom and dad to get back together."

Leo and I exchange glances. The day dad left, in a

great flurry of suitcases randomly stuffed with his clothes and books and toiletries, my sister showed a striking lack of interest. She even allowed herself the luxury of shooting one last razor-sharp *ciao* out the window at him.

"And grandpa," she adds, "I don't want you to die either."

"Okay," replies Leo, "I'm going to do what I can to pull through. Believe me, pussycat, I'd like that too."

"It's a deal," she says, seemingly appeased. Then she glances in my direction. "José, can I tell him my secret?"

I give her a disapproving frown. Jeanne doesn't arouse any sympathy in me. Furthermore, what with mom and dad's ever-shifting moods and E's invisible yet palpable presence, there's enough confusion here already.

"A secret?" Leo echoes softly. "Look, the bride-to-be has arrived."

Indeed, a car is braking after having crunched up the gravel driveway, and I can hear Lisa shout, "There's our little fiancée now."

"Come on, José, *please*," begs Miriam. "My secret'll help grandpa get better."

I think for a moment. She may not be wrong about that. Since Leo's had his attack, he seems to be obsessed with Jeanne. "Okay, go ahead," I end up saying.

She throws her arms around Leo's neck, whispers something in his ear, then comes back and sits next to me. The two of us wait. But Leo, who usually reacts so quickly, doesn't utter a word. He's just staring at the ceiling so intently that I automatically look up myself.

"Are you okay, Leo?" I ask after a minute of total silence.

His eyes finally come back down to us. "Thank you, my little darling," he says. "Thank you, kids. I'm going to sleep again for a while. See you later."

Once we're out in the hall, my sister buries her head in her hands.

"Miriam, why are you crying? You were right to tell him the news about Jeanne. It made him very happy."

"Oh José," she sniffles, "everything is too sad. I want to go back home and go to bed."

Having said that, she bounds down the stairs with her usual energy, but I follow her with my eyes, feeling vaguely worried. I have to tell mom to reassure Miriam as soon as possible. This whole damn weekend is nothing but bad news! We never should have set foot outside the house.

As I'm carefully shutting the door to the ghost room, I suddenly realize that Leo never did explain to me why Jeanne left.

Luc

I never really intended to leave the house or to leave them. It was just that the insidious tyranny Sarah exerted over me was humiliating, and her fits of rage wore me out. One Sunday night, solely because I came home a little late and had forgotten to tell her first, I found all my shirts, ties, and slacks shredded and stuffed in a garbage bag near the door. And when I would leave in the morning without saying goodbye, she would sometimes even throw my clothes out the window at me while the stunned neighbors looked on. But her imagination never ceased to amaze me—and mornings over coffee the little stories she occasionally told me while the children were still asleep would have me laughing till I cried. I admit that I too was guilty of losing my temper. At times I probably grew excessively violent, the way my father did. One night, beside myself with rage, I hit her. She had become hysterical, crying non-stop for three days, allegedly because of some trivial affair of mine with an Italian I met at a gallery opening, but when I hit her, she suddenly became icily calm. "I will never forgive you for that," she said. I felt ashamed, but, unable to put my despair into words, I kept still. If only I had known how to tell her that the mysterious, ineffable aura she radiated was driving me mad, she might have pardoned me. Only she wanted me at her beck and call, and that was out of the question. In spite of everything, I wasn't planning to leave. No, I just wanted to make a point and remind them all that I existed.

Everything blew up at the beginning of September, just after the first day of school. As I was coming home exhausted from a meeting in Tours, I could hear Miriam's favorite rock star's screechings from the street. Having made up my mind to teach my daughter a lesson, I rushed up the stairs. As I opened the apartment door, I was horrified by the staggering disarray that confronted me. When I saw Miriam vigorously swaying her hips amid heaps of random objects—summer clothes, notebooks, school books, cassettes—scattered everywhere, I blew my top, as José would say. I admit that in the throes of rage—justified as far as I'm concerned—I didn't mince words. And when, turning to Sarah as she languorously emerged from her office, I said something like, "I'm getting out of here—I've had enough of this madhouse," she didn't lift a finger to stop me. As three pairs of outraged eyes followed me, I was obliged to rummage through a closet stuffed to bursting just to get my hands on two duffel bags and an old suitcase, and in no time flat I found myself on the sidewalk left to wander the streets like a beggar.

I spent three months sleeping here and there at the home of anyone who would take me in. It was then that I discovered that Sarah's reputation as a novelist and her somewhat asocial character—let's call it her marginality—had won her not only friends, but also more than her fair share of enemies. She was envied for not being like everybody else but hated for that same reason. And if I tried defending her, people would reply with no little irony that she had certainly dumped *me* unceremoniously enough.

Every day I would wait for a sign from her, for one of those concise, well-formulated letters for which she has such a knack, but nothing ever came. Sarah, normally so lavish with words, had taken refuge behind an austere silence. Having been banished from the apartment, I would go pick up Miriam at school almost every day and flood her with questions, but she was a good little soldier who revealed nothing. Yes, her mother was doing fine and so was José, but never "Daddy, I miss you, please come home soon." She was so closed off to me that she wouldn't even turn around and wave when I'd drop her off at the corner. I was at the end of my rope—worn out, depressed—so I went to see Citrus.

"Your blood pressure is fine," he told me. "It's nothing serious, Luc. You've probably been working too hard, that's all."

"Dr. Citrus, what should I do?"

"Rest."

The good doctor was playing the innocent who's oblivious to everything. Knowing that he was basically well-meaning, I insisted. "But you know I'm in the street now, for God's sake. I'd like to be able to go home."

Slowly, Citrus closed my file. Then he took off his glasses and angled his chair toward his more than slightly grimy office window. "I understand, Luc," he said. "I understand. You know, ever since Sarah's mother left, she's lived in fear of being abandoned. I disapprove of slapdash psychologizing, but I suppose that unconsciously she provoked you precisely so she could prove to herself that no one can be counted on. It's strange, but human. Do you love her?"

His direct question caught me by surprise. "I don't know any more," I replied. "She and the kids are all united against me. Probably a part of me still loves her, yes."

It had been a long time since I'd been so honest and direct. The old Resistance fighter flashed a smile. "Well, in that case, my boy, tell her, because she doesn't know."

That same night, I met Erma at the home of one of my friends. I moved in with her the following week. Sarah's convinced I'd gladly make it with every nymphette on the planet, but in reality, I've only had a few brief affairs and, apart from Lisa, always with mature women, often even older than myself. I admit that Erma isn't a striking beauty. And she has neither the golden eyes nor that peculiar charm that characterizes my wife. On the other hand, she takes care of me, makes sure my clothes are clean, watches out for my health, and plans my weeks down to the most extraordinarily minute detail—to the point where I don't have a minute to dwell on my regrets any more. What's more, she makes love enthusiastically, and even if I imagine all too often that it's Sarah I'm holding in my arms, I try to convince myself I'm a lucky guy.

"Luc, there you are! We've been looking for you."

I must have nodded off while sunken into the drawing room couch, a whodunit in my hands. The voice of the one they call Billy brings me out of my half-sleep. Does he really have amnesia, this young man with the falsely innocent, blue-eyed gaze? Yeah, right. I can see it now. He's going to do his best to seduce Sarah—he's already started laying the groundwork—but at some point Lisa will corner him somewhere and make short work of him.

"What's up, Billy?" A first name straight out of a Western. Paul has a real talent for unearthing the strangest lodgers. The current one stares at me without answering. Suddenly I can't resist the temptation to add, "What's the problem, buddy—a temporary memory lapse?"

He just stands there, hands on hips, and doesn't react at all. All of a sudden, I hate him. He's young, handsome, athletic, and—above all—he's chosen to forget everything that might make him suffer. Unlike me, a man straightjacketed in his role as a man, a man I don't even recognize most of the time, who's constantly pretending to be someone he's not, Billy shines with the confidence that he has nothing to prove. His smooth face proclaims that knowledge. Indifferent to my sarcastic remark, he points toward the front lawn, now cloaked in the lengthening shadows of the late-afternoon twilight.

"Your son's looking for you—I'm just the messenger," he says, then slips away before I can even get to my feet.

Above my head in one of the upstairs bedrooms, I can hear several people talking excitedly. First Paul, who must have come back while I was dozing, then Lisa, who, for reasons that are not entirely clear, adores ceremonies of all kinds, and then a thin, reedy voice doubtless belonging to the bride-to-be. After knotting my sweatshirt around my neck, I go outside and look around the front lawn. Toward the back, near the big oak, I spy José standing with his hands in his pockets. He appears to be kicking at the ground impatiently. As I start walking over to him, I shout, "Joe! Joe, are you okay?"

I don't like the way he has his shoulders stiffly pulled back. He turns and looks at me without answering. Now that I'm close to him, I can see that his dark eyes are clouded with worry.

"Something wrong, José?"

"Yes, dad. And I don't know where mom has gone off to. The Austin has disappeared."

"You're worried about that? C'mon, you know she'll be back."

Now he's kicking at the ground again. "It's not her I'm worried about, dad. It's Miriam. She's lost it."

"What do you mean, lost it?"

He gives me a reproachful look. Everything's always my fault in this family. If one of them gets a cold, I'm the one they'll blame.

"Where is she, José? I'll go talk to her."

"Dad, don't you understand anything? I don't know where's she's gone. That's the whole point."

His tone is aggressive. The child who used to call me *mama* is filled with admiration for his mother and Leo, but I don't inspire his confidence. I hesitate before putting my hand on his shoulder. "Listen, Joe, before getting all excited, let's take a look around the château."

"But that's what I just got finished doing," he shouts. "I went through every inch of the place from basement to attic. I want mom to show up. Maybe she'll have an idea."

He's practically running now, and I have to take long strides just to keep up with him. Paul is standing on the front porch, smiling as he watches us approach.

"Good news, kids. Leo has finally come down, and he's looking fresh as a daisy. Right now he's cheering up our little Adeline—she's all shook up at the idea of getting married tomorrow."

José and I are both standing perfectly still as we wait for our host to finish talking. I finally murmur, "Paul . . ."

"What's happened? You both look upset."

As I'm about to explain, my eye catches his. Behind his affable demeanor, I sense a certain coolness. I suddenly wonder what he thinks of me. He once told me that Sarah had an exceptional talent and that it was my duty to nurture it. I've disappointed him, that's for sure. But who's ever nurtured me?

"Have you seen Miriam?" my son gasps hoarsely.

"No, not since I got back from Angers."

"You get it now, dad? She was feeling lousy, and now she's run away. We have to find her before it gets dark."

He's talking to me as if I were his worst enemy. I respond without conviction. "Look, José, she probably went with your mother." I should have thought of that earlier instead of getting caught up in his fears.

But Paul shakes his head. "Sarah went out to buy cigarettes at least half an hour ago. Alone."

José has already disappeared into the house. As I feel a lump forming at the back of my throat, making it hard for me to breathe, Paul says curtly, "That's all we need—a runaway. You abandoned your family, and now look what's happened. It's already getting dark. Where could that little girl be?" A tone of anxiety has crept into his voice.

Instead of admitting that I'm worried too, I declare firmly, "Wherever she is, I'll find her."

"Well, I certainly hope so."

Sarah

His parents, the Pottiers, used to live in this two-story house here on boulevard Foch. My father-in-law saw his patients in a dark, severe office that reeked of the little cigars he smoked from morning till night. His children feared his fits of rage, but I only saw him occasionally and liked him well enough. In the end I suffered for having a father who was beyond reproach. How could you get mad at Leo without seeming monstrously self-centered?

Luc's father, on the other hand, was easy to criticize. He was weak, fearful, quick to anger, and disinclined to work, but he lacked neither a sense of humor nor basic human kindness. On first meeting him, I discerned that he felt out of place in his universe. Sometimes I would sense such distress in his eyes that it would leave me feeling devastated. Toward the end of his days, he was so fed up with his life that he would go to bed at six o'clock every night. He had missed out on everything and knew it. Maybe that was why I found him so moving. But above all, he was the only person in the family who ever really accepted me. The others pretended to, but an indifference showed through their perfect manners, and that indifference made me retreat into an awkward silence.

Since Luc and I split up, I haven't heard from his brothers and sisters or from any of his countless cousins. Nothing, not a word. I've turned back into Sarah—that Jewish girl who's a novelist with no sense of family.

It's certainly strange. Here I was just driving to the next town for a pack of cigarettes, and I find myself in Angers in front of my in-laws' former house. Even if I haven't been able to endure his touch these last few years because I despised the change in him, the truth is he's rooted in me—and I can't do anything about it. And I know that, whereas I always wanted him to be different, he at least loved me as I was. God knows I didn't spare his feelings by being so uncompromising, sarcastic, disorganized, and disrespectful of his work, while so fiercely protecting my own. Naturally now that it's all over, I feel remorseful. How many times since he left have I sat at my desk in a vain attempt to whip up one of those funny little letters he used to find so amusing? Roughly one morning out of two. But it's hard to be funny when your own morale is shot. Without Luc around, I'm no longer able to write. In some way he was my muse. If it weren't for him, I would probably have produced only the one novel, yet I've never dedicated anything to him for fear of letting him see how much I depend on him. Now I'm going to be obliged to dig deep into my own entrails—that word would have Leo in stitches, since he finds it absurd to

talk about guts or entrails when discussing literature—
to find a new wellspring, another muse.

The shutters probably used to be some sort of
off-white but, not having seen the house since Luc's
parents retired to the coast, I can't remember the exact
color. In any event, whatever it was, they've been re-
painted blue. The house looks smaller to me than when
I endured my first comprehensive examination here.
Grade: decidedly below average. First of all, when I'm
intimidated, I either don't say a word or I start laughing in this maniacal cackle I can't control. Unfortunately, when it came time for my first meeting with
the Pottiers, it was my manic half that won out.

Luc had told his parents about my novel, the one
that moved its readers to tears, but hadn't uttered a
syllable about the comedian. And with good reason.
My employer was their bête noire, a person they would
have loved to strangle with their bare hands had they
not been afraid of catching some fatal disease in the
process. Now the two of us lampooned, among others,
bigots (my mother-in-law) and former collaborators
(my father-in-law). Bigoted collaborators: that was at
least a partial portrait of the senior Pottiers. Blind to
Luc's desperate winks, I spent the entire meal running
through the borderline-tasteless material I was writing
on a daily basis. As the after-dinner cheese was being
passed around and I was wiping the tears of laughter
from my eyes, I finally noticed that an eerie silence had
settled over the table. Suddenly realizing my blunder,
I proceeded to launch into a series of confused expla-

nations, rather than keeping quiet. I claimed that it was in spite of my profound reservations that I had been all but forced to work for the comedian because of his being one of my father's best friends. I suppose it was that last superfluous detail that permanently wrecked my relationship with my future in-laws. At that point Luc, unable to stand my tactlessness any longer, bluntly interrupted me to inquire about his cousins, the Delachaises—or some such aristocratic name. Dying of shame, I tried to pull myself together by gulping down a glass of vintage red wine. Unfortunately, I wasn't used to drinking, not even a single glass of wine, and within a minute I fainted dead away and fell out of my chair, landing violently against a fragile plant stand that held Madame Pottier's favorite vase. The subsequent crash reawakened me. I knew instantly that I'd committed an act of destruction for which Madame Pottier would never forgive me.

Before I could commit any further gaffes, Luc maneuvered me into his old Citroën, telling me curtly, "Now keep quiet." I sat there on the worn seat cursing Leo, thinking to myself that he had certainly done a poor job of teaching me how to cultivate people like the Pottiers. A tap at the half-open car window made me jump. The doctor was holding a red rose out to me. "To match the color of your cheeks, Mademoiselle Abner. And all the best to your employer on the part of a former collaborator." I stared at him dumbfounded. A slight smile was playing about the corners of his mouth. He bent toward me and whispered,

"You've done me quite a service. I always hated that vase."

Back at my house, of course, they laughed for weeks over my unfortunate experience, but each time I saw my in-laws again, I'd be sick with embarrassment and nervous dread as I recalled our disastrous first meeting.

"Are you looking for someone, madame?"

An old woman wearing a scarf around her head is walking up to the massive front door, a pair of pruning shears in hand. No doubt she wants to clip her rose bushes before it gets dark. I recall the smell of the red rose my father-in-law handed me as a peace offering. "No, not really," I hastily reply, "I knew the people who used to live here."

"Oh, that poor doctor," she says. "It's so sad."

But before she can launch into any pitying condolences, I quickly flee back into my Austin.

It's six at night and there are a lot of cars on the main route leaving Angers, so I look out for the back road leading to Echards. Everyone calls it "Paul's shortcut." It is, in fact, a couple of miles longer than the highway but infinitely prettier. The children are safe and sound back at the château, and I feel like taking my time.

Maybe I'll finally write the story of my father's side of the family—taking as my starting point another Lisa, the one who died giving birth to Leo, for example. She had a first cousin of exactly the same age. The cousin was also named Lisa and since they were inseparable, as soon as they would appear somewhere together walking arm in arm, the entire Jewish community of Kovno would say, "Here comes Lisa, Lisa."

After Leo told us that story, I took to calling my little sister Lisa, Lisa instead of that nickname—Zaza—that used to get her all worked up. "It makes me sound little, tiny," she would shriek in all her outraged six-year-old dignity. "I deserve to have a real first name like everybody else!" Shortly before starting high school, she suddenly decided that Zaza wasn't so bad after all. Oh how I coddled my sister, much more than I was ever to coddle either of my own children. By tacit agreement, Leo and I split up the duties. He took care of the theoretical end, I, the day to day. I can still see my little Lisa walking back white as a sheet from her first day of junior high school. Having gotten out of school before her, I had gone to meet her and was standing around waiting, discreetly smoking a cigarette. The minute I saw her, I shuddered apprehensively. She had gone to such pains to get ready that morning, so proud of finally being a big girl, and here she was returning so upset she was shaking visibly.

"What happened, Lisa? C'mon, talk to me."

Between sobs, she finally managed to say, "We had sewing class today. The teacher asked why my mom never showed me how to sew."

"So what did you say?"

"Nothing. I threw a notebook in her face, then ran

out of the room and slammed the door behind me. Now I'm going to be expelled because I don't have a mommy."

"Listen, Zaza, you won't be expelled. Leo'll take care of it. C'mon, I'll buy you a chocolate sundae at the Snack-Spot."

And of course, as always, Leo interceded with his usual panache. I never knew what he told our teachers, but my sister and I were always either mothered or treated with a respect that often bordered on fear. One way or another, it was always perfectly intolerable. To avoid being pitied, I would hedge, claiming that my mother was away on a trip, but Lisa would coldly declare that Jeanne was dead and buried. I told Jeanne all this when I saw her in Chicago. She cried as she listened to me, and I forgave her.

Since I've been living alone with José and Miriam, I think about my mother more and more often. Perhaps it's time we were all reunited. As soon as we get back to Paris, I'll call her to let her know that Leo isn't going to be around much longer. As for the airfare . . .

Lost in my own thoughts, I haven't noticed José rocketing toward me. Another few feet and I'd have run him over. "Hey, watch where you're going! Maybe you really are taking drugs after all. You've been truly impossible lately."

"But mom!" he shouts, and I see that he has tears in his eyes.

Leo hasn't made it. I was daydreaming along the way, musing over Luc, my in-laws, my next novel, and

I completely forgot about my father. I kill the motor, then let my head drop onto the steering wheel.

"Sarah, Leo's doing fine. He's sitting in the drawing room." It's Luc. He gently lays a hand on my head. "Wait, José," he adds. "Your mother doesn't know about any of this yet. Let me handle it, okay? Move over, Sarah, I'll park your car."

Feebly I murmur, "I don't understand. What's happened?"

From where we are at the foot of the driveway, I see them all lined up on the front porch, even Leo, who's leaning against a wall. Well, almost all of them. "Oh no, Luc, not Miriam! It isn't Miriam, is it?"

When he speaks, his voice has regained its former tenderness. "Don't be upset, my angel. Listen, she was feeling unhappy and she went for a walk. You know her. She isn't afraid of anything. José was hoping she was with you."

Now it's Paul's turn. He comes running up to open the car door for me. "I have army maps of the region. All we have to do is organize a systematic search. Since we have more than one car, we'll split up into teams and be sure to find her before nightfall."

If I weren't so worried, I'd be smiling at our host's panic-stricken expression. His hair has been mussed by the wind and is now standing straight on end, revealing his bald spot; he suddenly looks like a very old man.

"Are you sending us on a treasure hunt, Paul?" asks my father in a sarcastic tone.

I finally get out of the Austin on legs turned to jelly. "Well at least you're all right, Leo."

"It's all my fault, treasure. While I was telling my life story to José, our little pussycat was hiding behind the door. Something must have scared her."

"I know where she's trying to go," José breaks in.

"Where's that?" asks my sister.

"You're not going to like it, Lisa," my son replies in a toneless voice. "She's gone to see Jeanne."

My sister and I stare at him, stunned. "But Jeanne's in Chicago!" I burst out.

"No," replies Luc, "no, she's not. She came back to Paris a few months ago."

Lisa puts her hand to her throat. "And Miriam's seen her?"

Luc impatiently turns to José. "Explain it to them quickly. We don't have time to beat around the bush."

"Miriam's secret," our son mumbles without looking at anyone, "is that Jeanne comes and picks her up at school every day. She told me about it, and just now she told Leo too."

I'm unable to take it all in. Maybe I'll understand later when we've gotten Miriam back. But anything could happen to her at night. And I know just how afraid of the dark she is. At home she can't fall asleep unless her bedside lamp is left on. Doing my best not to burst into tears, I ask, "Has someone called the police?"

"Yes, I did," replies Adeline, the bubbly bride-to-be, a young woman with long brown hair.

Paul counts us with a trembling finger as if we were all children in a schoolyard. If this goes on much longer, he's going to start calling the roll. His voice is shaky. "I propose that we . . ."

"Come on," interrupts Luc, "I'll take Sarah and José, and the others can work it out among themselves."

"As for me," Leo chimes in, "I'll stay here with the housekeeper in case our little runaway decides to retrace her steps."

José is pulling me by the arm. "Can we get going now, mom?"

We've barely climbed into his station wagon when Luc peels out, tires squealing. I run a hand over the black leather seat and ask, "What make is your car?"

He smiles. "So you've developed a passion for cars now?"

"No, I'm just trying not to think about anything. That's all."

"Mom, you took an hour buying your smokes. You get lost or what?"

José is on the verge of hysteria. I realize only now that he watches out for his sister the way I used to watch out for mine. Maybe if I'd taken better care of them these last few months, none of this would have happened.

"No," I answer softly, "I went all the way to Angers to see what had become of your grandparents' house. You remember that rose your father handed me, Luc?"

"Yes. To match the color of your cheeks, Mademoiselle Abner."

"What, you heard that?"

I look at him. His dark eyes are shining with emotion. "Of course," he replies. "I have always heard everything."

José

"Oh, my José, I shouldn't have yelled at you on the driveway. I hadn't even noticed that I was back at the house already. You gave me such a fright running in front of me like that. You know how it is. My mind was elsewhere."

Mom's mind is always elsewhere when she's driving. The guy who gave her a license is a criminal. She tells the story herself of how she snookered him by telling Jewish jokes. He was too busy scribbling them down to watch her perform the maneuvers for the test. He even wrote her a note when she published her fourth novel, *Comprehensive Exam*. It went: *Bravo, Mademoiselle Abner, I got a good laugh out of your book. All the same, I hope that you have given up operating an automobile on a permanent basis.* It was signed: *An overly indulgent examiner.*

"What were you thinking about, mom?"

"Actually," she says in her melodious voice, "it's funny. I was thinking about Jeanne too."

I catch dad's eye in the rearview mirror. One Sunday morning as he was walking me to soccer practice, he said, "You know, growing up alone with Leo and

Lisa wasn't easy for your mother. So when her mind wanders, you have to be patient with her."

"You think that's why she writes books?"

"Might well be, Joe."

Mom's infamous books. I used to pick them up and flip through them, but I never had the slightest desire to read them. In the beginning I was too little, of course, but later I had some kind of mental block. And anyway, she's so dismal with titles that I tip my cap to her readers. I mean, who would buy a book called *Family Swallowed Whole* or *The Big Sister*? Talk about dull! When she tells anecdotes about people, she's always on target with little details that crack you up, but when it comes to book titles, she's truly clueless. She knows it, too, so she begs everyone to give her ideas, even Miriam . . . No, if I think about Miriam, I'm gonna flip out.

Good thing dad's driving slowly—it calms me down. The others must have fanned out along the back roads, but he took the highway in case she's decided to hitch to Paris. I can just see her in her red dress watching impatiently for cars—with her whole hand stuck out instead of just her thumb. Last summer when she ran out of steam riding her bike back from the beach, I got nowhere trying to explain proper hitch-hiking technique to her. My stomach's tied up in knots, and I don't even want to think about what might have happened to her.

But as for my mother's writing . . . I happened to be exposed to it by accident. My ninth-grade French teacher was a pretty wacky guy. He taught class from behind these dark sunglasses because he said the sight of us hurt his eyes. "Your stupidity is simply glaring," he'd say. Still, he was friendly and didn't grade too hard, so we all liked him well enough. Anyway, he was a real contemporary lit fan. He must've knocked off ten books a week. So one day he throws some passage at us to analyze. I start reading it and I'm saying to myself: *What is this mess?* The style was simple enough, no overly complicated words, but it was nothing but flashbacks jumping from here to there without rhyme or reason. There must have been ten different characters in those two pages, and all of them were half crazy to boot. A real jigsaw puzzle. I wasn't sure what to think, but I kept on reading and re-reading the passage. I was starting to get really tired of it when Ludo, who shared a desk with me at the time, elbowed me in the ribs.

"So'd ya see?" he whispered.

"What," I asked real quiet. "Oh yeah, right. I don't get this book at all."

At that point, Ludo started giggling.

"Is there a problem, my gifted ones?" asked Olivier, our teacher. (We called him by his first name; he was really cool on that front.)

"No, no," I answered. "No problem."

But there was Olivier coming over to me. "Do you have good eyesight, José?"

"Sure do. Twenty-twenty in each eye."

"Well in that case, look carefully at the end of this passage and read me the author's name."

"Must be another guy I've never heard of," I muttered. "Sometimes I wonder where you dig them up."

"Is that so? Guys aren't the only ones who write, m'boy. Go on, read."

He ran his finger down the length of the page, then pointed. Shocked, I discovered the name of the convoluted book's author: Sarah Abner.

My teacher had this really innocent look on his face. "Doesn't ring a bell?"

As my cheeks were turning positively crimson, I whispered, "No, it does. She's my mother. How'd you know?"

"I'm not as dumb as I look, m'boy. Anyway, you need not be ashamed of your mom. Her books are quite well constructed. A little confusing at first, but you get hooked as you go along. So, José, as a homework assignment, read *Family Swallowed Whole* for the end of the week. That's the novel this passage is taken from."

I started reading mom's novel on the sly that same night. And as soon as I'd finished the first one, I tore through all the others. It was like I was chasing after some elusive key to my mother's personality. So now, even if I don't have a clear-cut opinion about the literary merit of her writing, I do know what it's about. Her obsession—I knew this already, but I never would have dreamed she put it in her books—is the family.

Then, in no particular order, you have old men and teenagers, immigrants and foreign countries, trips, suicides and fatal accidents, nutsy mothers who abandon their children, incestuous fathers, and runaway children.

Turning to me, mom asks, "You okay, my José? You're being awfully quiet for once. It's not your fault, you know. Looking after her was my responsibility." Her voice falters. "My poor little darling."

"Don't get upset, Sarah," dad says for the tenth time.

But all three of us are thinking the same thing. Any random crazy could have picked her up, a sex fiend for example. Even now, when she goes traipsing down the street in her skintight jeans, some creeps leer at her— even though she's only nine.

"Mom?"

"Yes, José?"

"Who else in the family used to run away?"

She takes a drag on her cigarette before saying anything. "Why do you ask?"

" 'Cause in your books there's always a little girl packing her bags and hitting the road. Was it you?"

"No," she says softly. "Lisa. Practically every other month Leo and I would make the rounds of the hospitals and police stations."

"You think that has anything to do with Miriam? I mean, like, that it's some kind of genetic disease?"

"Maybe," she replies, "but who can say for sure?"

All I know about Lisa, and this only because Leo

told me, is that she tried to commit suicide when she was about the same age I am now.

I'm suddenly thrown forward. Dad has slammed on the brakes. A highway patrol car is blocking the road. I'm rushing out of the Ford in a panic before it even occurs to the parents to move. Behind two cops I can make out a white Porsche on the other side of the highway; its front end is completely smashed in. There's also a little Renault in pitiful shape lying in the ditch by the side of the road; judging by the way it's facing, it was going in the same direction we were.

"Nobody was hurt," says my father, sounding relieved.

I look around for my sister but can only make out two guys and a platinum blonde arguing loudly.

"Excuse me," interrupts mom, turning to the cops, "but did you happen to see a little girl with brown hair cut in a page boy that came down to here?" And with her hands she vaguely indicates her shoulders.

Dad, however, pulls a photo out of his wallet. "This little girl," he says.

The cops shake their heads. The accident victims have stopped arguing, and the photo is passed around.

"Now that you mention it, was your little girl wearing a red dress?" asks the platinum blonde.

"Where is she?" screams my mother.

"A mile or two from here at most. She was sitting by the side of the road when we went by. A tiny slip of a girl holding a big sign in her hands. I wanted to stop, but no, this genius here was in too much of a hurry. Now look what's happened." And she points scornfully at the Porsche.

"What was written on the sign?" I ask the woman.

She's staring at me. Her round blue eyes look like they're straight off a china doll. "That's right, I did notice," she says after thinking about it for a minute. "It said: GOING TO PARIS, 11TH ARRONDISSEMENT. THANK YOU."

That Miriam. At least sis has her head screwed on straight. Citrus lives in the eleventh right near our place. Maybe Jeanne's staying with him. I'd like to get more details from the blonde, but dad is pushing me and mom back to the car already.

"We have to hurry. There's still a chance of finding her where the woman saw her."

"Well, since you're pressed for time, get a move on," says one of the cops. "I'll pull my car over to the side of the road."

The three of us pile back into the Ford and dad takes off like a shot.

"Careful, Luc, you'll get us all killed."

"Look, Sarah, I know what I'm doing."

After about a mile, he slows down. It's completely dark now. Wherever she is, Miriam must be scared to death. At night, if she hears the slightest noise, she goes running for cover in mom's bed or in mine. We're going along at five miles an hour and my eyes are starting to burn from staring wide-eyed at the road and what's visible off to the side. But there's nothing—no red spot huddled by the embankment.

My old man sighs heavily. "I'm not quite sure what to do at this point. Anybody got an idea?"

As she lights yet another cigarette, mom gasps in a choked voice. "We've got to keep looking around here. You never know."

"Dad," I say in turn, "I think we'd be better off continuing on foot."

"You two are right," he says. "Maybe she went wandering away from the road."

He takes two flashlights out of the glove compartment and passes them to me and mom. I can tell he's as worried as we are, but his outward calm amazes me. I had gotten so tired of him for slamming doors and putting on such incredibly pouty looks that I'd forgotten how cool he is under pressure, even when the going gets really tough.

"I suggest we each head off in a different direction," he says. "Are you going to be all right, Sarah?"

He still loves mom—you can tell beyond a shadow of a doubt—and for once he's not ashamed to show it.

"Yes, of course," she answers.

I start walking down a little path. At the end of it I can make out a stream—the water is glittering under the full moon.

"Miriam? Miriam?"

Suddenly I trip over something. I aim my flashlight at the ground: it's Miriam's pink backpack, the one she sticks all her treasures in.

"Miriam, answer me! I know you're out there."

A splash in the water followed by a kind of muffled

cry leaves me practically choking with panic because Miriam has stubbornly refused to learn how to swim. Without thinking, I kick off my sneakers and dive, fully clothed, into the water.

"Please, Miriam, at least raise your hand. I can't see anything out here."

Silence. Then I hear dad's voice. "Did you find her, Joe?"

While I'm trying to swim as fast as I can in the direction of the splash, my mother's voice rises up right near me. "I'm the one who shouted, José." She aims her flashlight at the water, then adds: "Look, there's no one in there. Get out quickly; you'll catch pneumonia."

"But mom, I found her backpack. You know perfectly well she never lets it out of her sight." And, sure that my sister is tucked away somewhere nearby, I keep swimming toward the stream's invisible far shore. A whimper makes me jump.

"Miriam, is that you?"

"I can't raise my hand, José. My dress is caught on a branch. Come quick," she moans. "I'm about to fall in."

I've almost reached her but, walking along the opposite bank, my father has arrived ahead of me.

"Don't move, dearest," he says. "I'm going to get you untangled. Let yourself go, I'm holding you."

A few seconds later, she starts crying. "Daddy, tell me, am I the milkman's daughter?"

"What are you talking about?"

"Because if I am, I'd rather drown."

While hoisting myself up onto firm ground, I recognize the familiar sound of the Austin up on the road. A door slams.

"Sarah, yoo-hoo, Sarah. Somebody saw a little girl holding a sign." It's Lisa's voice.

After whispering "Thank you, my José" as she deposits a kiss on my forehead, mom replies, "We've found our little darling all safe and sound."

"Well, daddy?"

Now Miriam's starting that up again. When that girl gets an idea in her head, she sticks to it.

"Well *what*?"

"So whose daughter am I?"

"Why, mine, for Chrissake, my one and only daughter, the girl I love more than any other. Do you think I'd lie to you?"

Silence. "I don't know. Everybody lies, especially grown-ups."

In the darkness, I can see that dad has picked her up. "We're going to get you dried off," he says softly, "and make you a big mug of warm milk, and then the two of us will have a little talk. Okay?"

"Okay!" my sister says solemnly. "Okay!"

Luc

The children's teeth are chattering with cold. In the back seat Sarah has an arm around each one of them and as they cuddle against her, she whispers soothing words to them. I'm envious. If it weren't for that intolerable Billy behind us in the Austin, I would be perfectly happy for the first time in a long time. Today they haven't criticized or humiliated me; they've let me take care of them, and I'm grateful for it.

My family. They're much closer to me than my own parents, those strangers who brought me into this world. Because of my reluctance to express my feelings clearly—thank God neither José nor Miriam takes after me in that regard—I have never admitted to Sarah that I practically burst out laughing the day of her unforgettable performance that first time in Angers. Thanks to her, I finally felt liberated from the family straight-jacket, felt I was leaving far behind me those hateful traditions, that mix of social conventions and accepted ideas, that horrible ignorance of the outside world that seemed to imply that they were the only ones on earth in possession of the truth. Or rather, of the *proper* way to live. You acted properly at marriages and at funerals; you knew exactly what was to be said to each person;

and that was good enough. You were content. And as for other people who didn't conform to the sacred rules, they could drop dead. With them, women didn't have first names. Couples were called the Lucs or the Jeans or the Pierres, and so forth. Sarah was never able to stomach that custom, and I must say I can understand why.

I left home as early on as possible, at the age of eighteen, because I hated my parents' relentless pride in their pedigree—and their rigidity. Why then have I put myself under the thumb of a woman like Erma? Probably because she spells everything out precisely and organizes her mind with such brutal efficiency that no room is left for imagination, dreams, or the irrational. It's also too dangerous to let myself spend an evening alone with my children. If I insist on not seeing them without Erma, it's probably because I'm afraid of their judgment and prefer knowing nothing, hearing nothing.

Suddenly giddy with thoughts of revolt, I imagine Sarah and Erma meeting. That would really be a scream. Exactly the kind of incident Sarah would stick in one of her novels. If that novel isn't already in progress! I'm suspicious.

She's already pulled that trick on me once. This was a few years ago—what a nightmare. Generally her stories are pure inventions. Oh sure, you can find bits and pieces of this or that person, but always in a different form. Only this time, she did the opposite. Her book's two main characters were none other than my best friend Maxime and me. Our conversations, our drinking binges, our off-color anecdotes—it was all in there, verbatim. She hadn't bothered to disguise anything whatsoever—not our professions, not our physical appearances, not our annoying habits, not even our voices. The one who was supposed to be Maxime was a painter and my character was an architect. It was really very funny; we both came across as blithering idiots. Two pathetic guys closing in on forty who speak pretentiously about their jobs, self-indulgently about their conquests, and pompously about the world at large. She really had us pegged that time. I should have suspected she was up to something of the sort since this was the one time I was exempted from my usual reading chores during the gestation process. But naturally the scales fell from my eyes when, as she handed me a first printing of the novel, she told me, "Luc, you mustn't get angry. I just wanted to have a little fun. You get so few chances to have a really good laugh in this life, right?"

Once I got over the initial shock, I didn't take it too badly. When you live with a novelist, you're necessarily running a risk, and until then I had been spared. But Maxime was positively livid. For weeks he tried in vain to have Sarah's novel impounded and after that he never spoke to her again. Not a single word, even though his apartment is in the next building over. She was shocked and very sad because she genuinely adores Maxime.

"I don't understand, Luc. He has such a good sense

of humor. It's really stupid of him to get angry about some trivial little novel."

"That's just it, Sarah. That's exactly the way you portrayed him: a trivial little idiot with no balls. He thinks you've betrayed him."

"But when the two of you are alone together, you really are a bit like that. Frankly, I'm always amazed when I overhear you. Two men who are individually very amusing, and suddenly, the minute they start pontificating, they turn into this deadly dull duo. You sound exactly like two little boys pretending to be grown-ups. I'm telling you, I've often regretted not having a tape recorder around when you two go at it."

Vintage Sarah Abner. Instead of admitting she's gone too far, she raises the stakes. I must have been in a particularly good mood that day, because all I did was sigh. "No need for a tape recorder now. Everyone's going to recognize us. What a pleasant thought."

In a burst of unaccustomed tenderness, she threw her arms around my neck. "Well, in that case you'll be famous. Isn't that what you want? Anyway, you're taking it with style. But I simply do not understand Maxime. And to think I once considered him my best friend. We've had such good laughs together, he and I. And you'd think that as a painter, he'd understand. Why, if he ever asked me to pose for him, I'd do it in a flash. I don't see what all the fuss is about."

She was being sincere, no doubt. I promised to put in a good word for her with my friend, but every time I saw Maxime, I would mysteriously forget to bring up the painful subject. She was upset with me about that, no doubt thinking once again that I was a coward . . .

We finally make it back to the château. Some-one, probably Paul's housekeeper, has turned on the yard lights. Leo is standing bolt upright on the top step of the front porch, his ever-present flask in hand. Blinded by my headlights, he puts a hand to his eyes before exclaiming, "Have you found our pussycat?"

Miriam goes bounding out of the car bare-bottomed. She's grown so much these last few months that my sweatshirt only comes down to her waist.

"Grandpa," she calls out in her booming voice, "you *were* worried about me, I hope?" Impulsively she throws her arms around his neck. He hugs her tightly.

"No, my darling, I wasn't worried at all. In fact, I congratulate you. Going out for a walk in the middle of the night was an excellent idea. Eminently reason-able."

As Sarah gives her father a dirty look, José ex-claims, "Oh, really! Then what the hell was she doing in a stream if she's so reasonable?"

"I'm telling you, grandpa, I didn't want to drown. I wanted to find Jeanne, but my sign was so teensy that the cars wouldn't stop for me. So I started walking through the grass. Then I didn't see the stream 'cause it was all dark out and I fell right in. After that, José called me."

"Come on, kids," Sarah says, "it's time to go inside and put on some dry clothes. Papa, the others aren't back yet?"

When the hour is dark, Leo once again becomes *papa* to his daughters.

"No, treasure, it's rather complicated. I believe Paul said he would telephone every hour. He should be calling any minute now."

Suddenly I see the Austin hurtling toward us at breakneck speed. Since Lisa appears to be charging straight at my Ford, I try to motion her to the side. Too late. As she's finally coming to a stop in a terrific screech of tires, she succeeds in scratching the right front door of my brand-new car. All around me, everyone bursts out laughing. The man without a memory is the first one out of the Austin. In the darkness, I can't make out his expression, but I feel as if I'm being transfixed by his insolent gaze.

"Just a little scratch," he declares before adding: "I'm going to see if the kids need me."

I shrug my shoulders in exasperation. This Yank is probably no more of a doctor than I am.

"A thousand pardons, Luc," gasps Lisa, who then turns to Leo. "Papa, were you able to get in touch with Citrus?"

"Yes. As soon as I heard Luc's car, I called him back. They're taking the eight o'clock to Angers."

"They? What do you mean *they*?" She's practically screaming.

Leo brushes a single finger along his daughter's cheek. "He and Jeanne."

"Oh, no. No, no, no, I don't want to see her. That

bitch! That slut! If that's the way it's going to be, I'm leaving."

"Lisa, you aren't the one who's nine years old," Leo replies sternly. "Are you going to run away the way you used to? Don't you think your sister and I spent enough sleepless nights wandering the streets of Paris looking for you! It's high time you faced reality. You will simply have to settle the score with your mother here and now."

I've never heard him speak so bluntly to Lisa. Unlike Sarah, whom he often teases, he's generally mindful of his younger daughter's feelings, aware that she is the more sensitive of the two. Lisa chokes back a sob and disappears into the château, leaving me alone with my father-in-law.

"Lot of work?" Leo asks after taking a few sips from his flask.

"Oh, yes. I'm in it up to my neck as usual. You know, I kept meaning to find out how you were doing, but . . ."

"But you were afraid I might ask you some embarrassing questions."

"That's one way of putting it, yes."

He clears his throat. "Citrus told me you were devastated. I'd never allow myself to pass judgment on you, but I was surprised you were so quick to move in with another woman. Are you really that afraid of being alone?"

I silently contemplate the cloudy sky for a moment. Perhaps it's his approaching death or Jeanne's impending arrival, but for whatever reason Leo, normally so full of tact, isn't going at it with the blunt edge of the sword tonight. From inside the house I can make out Miriam's resounding voice. I promised I'd talk to her and, knowing her as I do, I can imagine the way she's impatiently waiting for me. "Could be," I reply softly.

"I'm afraid too, you know, but for other reasons. Do you realize that I haven't seen Jeanne for thirty-three years now? Thirty-three years." He repeats the words dreamily. "Go ahead, I want to stay outside a minute and breathe the night air."

There's no one in the drawing room or the dining room, but my wife's serene voice comes wafting over to me from the kitchen. Without making any noise, I cross the laundry room. The two sisters are sitting side by side on the wooden bench by the breakfast table. Sarah has put her arm around her little sister, whose delicate features are distorted with worry.

The floor creaks. The two of them raise their heads as one. Without relaxing her embrace, Sarah proclaims, "Luc, it's you. I never hear you coming. You're as silent as ever."

"Miriam's upstairs?"

"Yes. She drank some warm milk here with us, and now Billy is reading *The Little Prince* to her."

Billy, of course. When it isn't Leo or José, there's always someone else available to take my place with my daughter.

"Well, I'm going up."

"Luc," Sarah whispers in her most innocent voice.

"Yes, Sarah?"

"Good luck."

On the upstairs landing, I run into José on his way out of the bathroom wrapped up in a thick white towel.

"Gotten warm, José?"

"Yeah, dad. If you're looking for Miriam, she's in the little blue bedroom."

The one I used to sleep in as a kid when I'd come spend the weekend here. My son is looking at me.

"You okay, dad?" he asks.

Touched by his concern, I reply, "Of course I am."

When I come to the door to the blue bedroom, I hesitate before giving two light taps.

"Who is it?"

How is it that Miriam's voice is so willful? I suddenly picture her commanding an infantry battalion.

"It's me," I say, then walk into the room without further ado.

My daughter is curled up in a ball on the narrow bed. I can only see one of her eyes. Billy flashes an enigmatic smile and stands up. As he closes the book he's holding in his hand, he murmurs, "I'll leave you two alone. See you later, Miriam."

Once he's departed, I sit down on the side of the bed. "You see. I've come just the way I promised."

She solemnly nods her head. Her fine hair is still wet. I want to reach out and stroke her head but don't dare. Something is holding me back.

"So tell me, Miriam, what's this business about the milkman?"

She looks at me. "I dunno. That was something José told me. I didn't really get it anyway. Daddy, do you love E more than mom?"

"It's different, my darling."

"And what about me and José?"

"Why, you're my children."

"So how come we never see you any more?"

"But don't you remember? I used to come pick you up at school almost every day. You wouldn't even say goodbye to me. That made me feel bad, you know."

"Well, if you had kept coming, I would have said goodbye to you. But ever since you started living with her, you stopped loving me any more. I'm sure she doesn't want you to see me."

"But Miriam . . ."

Waving me off imperiously, she interrupts. "Besides, if she told you to jump out a twelfth-story window, you'd do it. I said that to José."

Horrified by the implications of her example and staggered by her bluntness, I am left speechless for a moment.

"Well, daddy, cat got your tongue?"

It'll be a cold day in hell before the cat gets Miriam's tongue. One day not long after I moved out, I asked her in front of her school if she wanted me to come back home, and she shot right back with: "All that stuff is your business, not mine; *I'm* not a divorce lawyer."

Hiding my distress, I go on. "And what did José have to say to that?"

She smiles in spite of herself. "He said, 'Well, maybe not from a twelfth-story window.' "

"My darling, do you really hate Erma that much?"

Her answer is immediate. "Oh yes. She's so dumb. And she's always ordering you around. Do this, do that, and you go along with it like a good little doggy. When mommy used to ask you to do something, you'd always tell her to bug off."

No use explaining to Miriam that in her own way, Sarah is every bit as demanding as Erma. The judgment my daughter has passed on me leaves me feeling devastated. It's true that I watch my step around Erma. Because she took me in when I was at the end of my rope? To hide the fact that I don't really love her? I don't really know myself. Just as I'm about to break down in front of my daughter, she reaches out her little hand to me.

"Daddy, you look sad."

I feel my throat tighten. "Sometimes grown-ups don't know quite what to do," I murmur weakly.

"Yes," she says, "I understand. Is it true that José used to call you *mama* when he was little?"

"How did you know that?"

" 'Cause he told me. Will you make me spaghetti carbonara tonight?"

"Of course, my darling."

And finally I embrace her.

Sarah

I've finally managed to comfort my sister. As when she was a little girl and then a teenager, Lisa thinks only of fleeing at the prospect of confronting the unknown. And of course, more than anything else in this world, the woman who's coming in from Chicago after so many years represents the unknown, with all the doubt and menace that term implies. Nevertheless, I'm sure that Lisa's periodic disappearances were with only one goal in mind: finding the mother who had abandoned her.

"Listen, Lisa, you mustn't panic. Don't forget that the choice is yours now: you can ignore her, be civil to her, insult her, whatever. She's the one with the unpleasant part in this business. Put yourself in her place."

"I refuse to put myself in her place."

Her voice has not regained its usual liveliness, but beneath my fingers I can feel her shoulders loosening up. "Acting as my mother wasn't too hard on you?" she asks me quietly. "I sure put you through a lot, didn't I?"

"Not at all, my Zaza. Quite the contrary. I was

very proud of myself for taking care of you. It made me feel useful."

And now all sorts of memories come flooding back, a host of incidents—some funny, some sad, some frankly tragic—that have marked my life. It's my mother's return that has touched off this upheaval. Strangely enough, unlike Leo and Lisa, who feel frantic at the thought of seeing her, I feel cold, practically detached. This weekend is beginning to resemble one of those monologues I used to write. Or some utterly tasteless vaudeville act. All that's missing to make the scene complete is Erma. Then the situation would turn into a full-fledged farce. I let out a little laugh.

"What is it, Sarah?" Lisa asks, looking at me out of the corner of her eye.

"Oh, nothing."

"No, it's something. I know you. Deep down, you find this whole situation funny."

Her cheeks have regained their normal color. When all is said and done, even if matters have been rather hectic these last few hours, all is really going quite well. Leo seems to be holding up; we found Miriam before it got completely dark; Luc is being wonderfully kind; and my mother is coming back after a long absence.

"You're right," I admit to my sister. "I was thinking that we'd be right in our element in an insane asylum. Starting with Leo. After all, he could have gone looking for Jeanne. All he had to do was get on a plane, but he never did. Why? Because he was too proud or too manipulative. He preferred playing the victim."

"Like you, Sarah?" she says, using her most innocent tone.

I shrug my shoulders. "Hey, how about showing a little respect for your older sister. My problems with Luc are my business. Want me to tell you something that's gonna make you laugh?"

She's smiling already. I get up and open the fridge. "How about something to drink? Look, Paul has a bottle of Chablis."

As I'm searching for a corkscrew, the French doors leading from the kitchen to the back yard open, and Paul and Adeline appear.

"What a relief," our host declares. "I was terribly worried about your daughter, Sarah."

He doesn't appear relieved at all. Leo probably just informed him that Citrus is coming with Jeanne, and he must be feeling overwhelmed by events. Much too much upheaval for a spring wedding. As he stares at Lisa and me, he's probably wondering how we can look so calm.

"I didn't know anything about the business with your mother," he finally sighs. "That damned Citrus could have told me what was up. Of course I'm thrilled at having them."

Adeline puts on a radiant expression.

Turning to her, I murmur, "Adeline, I'm so sorry about all this commotion. I hope we haven't spoiled your wedding for you."

At those words, Paul rolls his eyes in exasperation.

"That's just it," the girl chirps in her sparrowlike

voice, "I've thought it over. I'm not getting married after all. Uncle Paul is most displeased."

"Someone has to inform that unfortunate young man," Paul thunders, "and don't count on it being me, little girl. Now where has Marie gotten herself off to?"

Marie is the housekeeper-cook who's been keeping the château running for at least twenty years.

"She's resting," says Lisa.

"But who's going to make dinner?"

He suddenly looks so troubled that I feel the need to reassure him. "Why, we will—Lisa, Luc, and I, that is. Don't worry about it, Paul. Can we have a bit of your Chablis?"

"Sure, sure. As for you, Adeline, hurry up and make your phone call. I'm going upstairs for a quick nap. All this excitement has worn me out."

Sitting across from one another, wineglasses in hand, my sister and I watch them file out of the kitchen.

"Chalk up another one to the Abner virus," says Lisa. "The little cousin, I mean. When the whole lot of us go somewhere together, it's chaos. So, you had a funny story to tell me?"

"Oh, I don't know if it's so funny after all. You remember all those letters I wrote for my friends back in high school?"

"You even wanted to write them for me. What a mess! No chance I'd forget about that."

I was fourteen or fifteen years old. High schools

weren't coed at the time, and practically all of us were obsessed with the boys we'd run into on the street or in local cafés. Because they were even more timid than we were, they hesitated to approach us unless they were in a group, and even then it was only to tease us. I proposed an extremely simple solution to my little classmates. If the boys weren't even going to risk asking us out for a cup of coffee, probably for fear of being embarrassed by a refusal, we would each write to the object of our heart's desire. But since none of *them* dared compose love letters, I was named class scribe by acclamation. Unfortunately, this was all happening at a time when, fed up with reading the classics, I had just discovered Henry Miller. I tried to match the tone of my letters to each girl's personality, but on the whole, the diction was terribly crude. In fact, responding to some devilish urge, I took particular delight in writing of stiff pricks and slimy cunts. Was it group hysteria or man-hating at an early age? In any event, rather than protest, my classmates mostly just snickered as they copied down the unseemly phrases I submitted for their approval. Of course, what I was writing was so repugnant that none of us ever got any response. My pornographic literature ruined us with the guys at the neighboring boys' school for two solid years. But I had a lot of fun and was thrilled with my joke.

Unfortunately, the story didn't end there. One night around seven, as I was telling Lisa some foolish story, Leo, contrary to his principles, came bursting into our room without knocking. "Sarah, stop that yapping. I have to talk to you. Come into the dining room."

His Russian accent was particularly pronounced, which with him is a sign of either agitation or anger. As I cast a surprised look at my sister, I wondered what could be the matter—Leo almost never got angry. I followed him into the dining room. There next to the bread basket on the table was a sheet of paper I had no trouble recognizing. It was obviously one of those infamous letters.

"Are you pleased with yourself?"

I decided to deny everything across the board. "Did you get some bad news, papa?" I replied casually.

"Sarah, don't play smart with me. And for God's sake, stop fidgeting and sit down. Read this abomination!"

He handed me the letter. Casting my eyes over it, I recognized the tiny handwriting of Evelyne Rolin, one of my most shameless classmates. Indeed, it was she who had copied out my racy prose with the most gusto. But who had been the recipient of her letter? As Leo was silently observing me, I was wracking my brain. Suddenly I remembered to my horror that she had sent it to the son of a couple who lived on our very floor. Apparently the boy's cynical detachment had irritated her.

"Gotten your memory back, my girl?"

Realizing that it was going to be useless to try and hedge, I feebly replied, "Yes, papa."

Leo's lively eyes were blazing. "It would have to be the Duchemins who are mixed up in this. The whole damn family hates us already because we're Jewish."

"And they realized that it was me who . . . well, who . . ."

I was on the verge of tears. Leo had done his best to raise us to be good girls, and here I had gone and betrayed him.

"They came together to visit me at the plant. 'Only Sarah Abner could come up with filth like this,' they said. 'She'll end up in the gutter.' They went to your little friends' parents first, and she evidently let the cat out of the bag."

Evelyne had snitched.

"Papa, are you going to send me away to boarding school?"

My question was thoroughly disingenuous. I knew that Leo would never part with us.

"Me? What an idea. But your sense of provocation worries me. You'd do anything to be noticed. Writers are free to write whatever they want—I'm opposed to any form of censorship—but Sarah, you're just a girl. I don't know what I'm going to do with you. Just now I even asked Citrus if it might not be necessary to send you to one of those people who treat the mind."

He must have been distraught to have had an idea like that! The slightest reference to psychoanalysis normally raised his hackles.

"Well, what did Dr. Citrus say?"

A wry smile finally came to Leo's lips. "He didn't

say anything. He just laughed. Tell me, Sarah, what do you want to do when you're old enough to have a real job?"

I'd never thought about the future in any kind of concrete way, and yet my answer was immediate and unequivocal. "I want to be a writer."

Maybe I was punished. I honestly don't remember any more. But shortly after the dirty-letters episode, Lisa ran away yet again—and Leo forgave me for having caused him shame . . .

Night has descended on the château. My sister lights one of my cigarettes and settles into her chair. "What made you think of those letters?" she asks. "That sure was a long time ago."

"Because I recently started up again."

"And who was the lucky recipient?"

I gnaw at my lips before answering. "Luc. But I sent the letter to his lady-love. I suggested some three-handed fun—you get the idea. I wrote it on Leo's electric typewriter and signed it *a secret admirer*."

Instead of laughing, Lisa looks at me with dismay. "Honestly, Sarah, you come up with some real winners! If you wanted Luc to come back home, that was the last thing you should have done. You know perfectly well he must have figured out right away who the secret admirer was. That woman of his must think you're an absolute nut case."

"Yes, I know. It wasn't very smart of me."

"Who's a nut case?"

Billy has materialized out of nowhere. He pours

himself a little wine, leans against the wall, and watches the two of us with his strangely pale, indeed almost transparent, blue eyes.

"My big sister," says Lisa.

The young man without a memory falls silent. Suddenly I envy him. When he has to come face-to-face with his mother, he'll be able to greet her just like that without having a heap of resentment clouding his judgment. I can hear his vaguely drowsy voice saying hello—and I see his cold, detached gaze. As for me, when I'm face-to-face with Jeanne, as I soon shall be, I'm sure to fall apart even if I do my best to keep my mind elsewhere. I'll be thinking of the thousand and one times I felt like dying because I was so sad about not having a mommy. I'm already getting teary. Paying no attention to Billy, I murmur, "Lisa, I'll be right back to help with the cooking. I'm going to look in on the kids."

"You wish we could trade places, Sarah, yours for mine?"

This amnesiac is a mind reader. "Yes, that's it precisely, Billy," I reply, irritated by his composure. "And since you know everything, how about telling me exactly what time Leo's going to die?"

"Sarah!" gasps my sister. "Have you lost your mind?"

Billy stares at me without answering and, probably disconcerted by my brutal question, follows me into the drawing room, where José is watching TV all alone.

"Where have the others gotten off to?" I ask him.

"Flew the coop, mom. Don't look at me like that. They're upstairs in the bedrooms. Dad's talking to Miriam, Adeline's explaining to Leo why she's not getting married any more, Paul's mad as a wet hen, and the housekeeper's got a migraine. Me too, as far as that goes. And I'm also starving."

"Listen, José, I have something to discuss with Billy in private. How 'bout leaving us alone for a minute?"

My son gives me an outraged look. "No way. I'm old enough to hear."

"Certainly old enough to be obnoxious."

"You don't have to shout, mom. Everybody will think we have another missing person case."

"I'm not shouting, José."

"Want me to get you on tape?"

Billy is perched, arms folded, on the side of one of the armchairs. "Well Sarah?" he cuts in.

Without benefit of a preamble, I get right to the point. "Why did you tell me you were from Chicago?"

"Because it's the truth."

His face doesn't betray the slightest trace of emotion. Maybe he's taken us all for a ride and he's neither a doctor nor an American. Maybe he's not even suffering from amnesia.

"My mother also lives in Chicago. Don't you think that's a pretty weird coincidence?"

"Mom," José whispers, "chill out. You're blowing this way out of proportion. It's not his fault."

But Billy just stares at me impassively. "Maybe it

is weird, but there's nothing I can do about it. This morning I didn't even know Jeanne existed. Is the interrogation over?"

He may not have shown any emotion, but I've probably hurt his feelings. Embarrassed, I reply in a kinder tone, "Yes."

And before I can add that I'm sorry for getting carried away, he's disappeared.

"Way to go, mom. If he goes and packs his bags, Paul's gonna kill us. You sure have a light touch when you put your mind to it!"

"Okay, so I was wrong. I'm not myself today. I feel completely drained."

José settles back into his armchair, shrugs his shoulders, and says, "Speaking of drained, my stomach . . ."

"Yes, José, I know. You're hungry. Couldn't you turn the TV down a little?"

"No, I need the noise to brighten up the atmosphere around here."

When I glare at him, he finally smiles at me. "Okay, fine. I'll turn it down if it'll make you happy. Say, mom, you think we're going to have to wait till they get here to eat? I mean till Citrus and . . . well—"

"Your grandmother. No, not to worry, we'll eat before they get here."

"What am I gonna call her? Madame or something?"

"I don't know, José. Whatever feels right, I guess."

He heaves a heavy sigh. "I should have said something to you when Miriam told me she was coming to pick her up at school. Apparently she wanted to see me too."

"Didn't appeal to you?"

"No, not really. But one day I went to have a look all the same."

"And?"

"They walked right by me, but I was out of sight. You know, she really looks like you there." He points to the top half of my face.

"I know," I reply. "Friends of Leo's seeing me for the first time would always gape."

My son hesitates before laying his hand on mine. In his expressive look, I can make out all sorts of feelings: tenderness, compassion, curiosity. "What's it like having her come back this way, mom?"

"It's no big deal."

"Oh, come on, tell me!"

"Well, it makes me think that if she had stayed, I might have been a different person. A better one."

As I'm getting up, he murmurs, "You're not so bad the way you are, mom." Then he falls back into his armchair. All I can see now is the thick fringe of hair that comes down to his eyebrows. Suddenly the misplaced sound of the television explodes through the château's drawing room.

José

I don't know why I asked dad if he was okay when I ran into him at the top of the stairs just now. He looked all upset about having to face Miriam's questions, and I've gotta admit I understand why. She adores him, but when she tries to get to him, she sure doesn't miss her mark.

What do I feel for him? I get butterflies in my stomach just thinking about it. See, used to be my father was the only guy I wanted to be like when I grew up. But I don't have too many illusions about him any more. Maybe you can count on him in a pinch—I guess he showed that when we were searching for Miriam. That was no act. But what choice did he have? Wasn't like he was going to sit around the château twiddling his thumbs, now was he? All right, I'm exaggerating. But I'm definitely fed up with him, and for a whole bunch of reasons.

When he was still living at home, it was mom who made all the important decisions, especially the ones having to do with us kids. Toward the end there, he'd always have a million and one reasons for slipping out—a problem at the office, a deadline for a competition, a conference, or one of his goddamned social obligations.

(You really had to hear the pompous way he'd say that last one; he couldn't have been any snootier if he'd tried.) And now to top it all off there's Erma; I'm sure she doesn't hesitate to tell him exactly what she thinks of us. Personally I tend to be pretty cool with people, *tolerant* as Leo would say. But without being openly rude, around this lady I'm about as warm as an iceberg. See, I can sense just how much she hates us. Sometimes I tell myself that it's because of her that my father has forgotten that Miriam and I even exist. As soon as we're out of sight, we're way out of mind. In fact, I've been thinking that I'm going to be the one to look out for my mother and sister when Leo's dead.

Just before I went downstairs, I took a minute to browse in peace in Paul's study, a very narrow room with walls lined floor to ceiling with books. I've always loved that room. It reminds me of mom's study in Paris—because of the smell of books and the stillness. The atmosphere there is so calm you'd think you were right in the middle of the desert. All that's missing are the camels. Sitting there I'd all but forgotten that everywhere else in the house people were throwing fits, with the exception of my grandfather, who almost never gets worked up. Judging by the outbursts I could hear coming from Paul's room, our friend would have been better off breathing in some of the calm in his study instead of ranting at his little cousin. He's mad at Adeline because her decision not to get married is the straw that broke the camel's back, as they say; but

I'm sure that if he weren't too polite to kick us all out, he'd do it gladly. It's true there hasn't been a dull moment since we came. I'd even say we've been pretty impressive when it comes to drama and disaster. But considering how long Paul's been friends with Leo, you'd think he'd be super used to it by now.

When I recognized my grandfather's voice, I hunched down and put my ear to the ground.

"Look, my dear Paul," he was saying, "the little lady is making a brave decision. It amazes me how sensible she is."

"If she's so sensible," screamed Paul, "she could have cancelled everything a month ago when there was still time. What am I going to do with all this fruit juice? It's not like you're going to drink it."

"Ah well, dear comrade, I'll bend my normally strict dietary rules to be of service to you. We'll swill fruit juice together like a couple of old health nuts."

At that point Paul started screaming even louder. "Jesus Christ, can't you and your family keep calm when you all go somewhere together?"

I could just imagine the scene: Paul purple with rage, my grandfather placidly sipping his whiskey.

"I don't understand you, Uncle Paul," Adeline slipped in. "You're asking them to keep calm, but personally, I'm convinced that what you like about them is that they're *alive*, for God's sake. You love the way they cry and laugh and carry on. Watching them today, I had this flash; I realized I couldn't go and bury

LISA, LISA

myself alive in Angers. Not with a lawyer! Philippe is so boring—he never raises his voice, ever. Would you rather see me unhappy?"

Adeline has a funny way of expressing herself. She talks so fast her sentences run together. It's hilarious listening to her. Personally I think she's a riot. She's not exactly beautiful, but she's awfully cute with her long dark hair, pink cheeks, and firm little body. And above all she has great breasts, nice and round—the kind I'd love to get my hands on.

I've always preferred girls who were older than me. Even when I was a kid, I used to love to sit on the laps of Lisa's girlfriends and breathe in their scent. Mom teases me about liking brunettes like Caroline, my girl-friend. But Caroline's a drag. The other day at the movies when I wanted to kiss her, she started squealing like I'd tried to rape her. And I'd even paid her way. At least twenty-year-old girls don't put up so much fuss. Maybe I should try my luck with Adeline, seeing as she thinks so highly of all of us.

Anyway, I can't complain too much. Nobody in the family knows it—it isn't the kind of news I'd go shouting from the rooftops—but I'm not a virgin any more. And indirectly it's thanks to dad, which is really pretty funny.

At the end of the summer, Ludo and I took a serious look at the situation. Naturally we'd been counting on summer vacation, but the first day of school was fast approaching, and the two of us were unchanged, still as pure as Jesus on the cross. We hung out in our usual café, the Switchblade, and caucused.

"You got a plan?" Ludo asked me as he lit up a Marlboro. He started smoking last year. "I'm sick of beating off to trashy porno mags. I'm afraid I'll go blind."

He was only half joking. Ludo's parents are the uptight kind when it comes to sex. ("They must have fucked only twice in their entire miserable lives," says my pal. "Once for me and once for my brother.") Ludo finds it humiliating that his mother inspects his sheets almost every morning. It would never even occur to mom to do something like that. Apart from a few jokes about the guys Lisa's making it with, we almost never discuss sex. We'd both die of embarrassment. But around the time I turned eleven, she sat down on the side of my bed one night. "Say, my José, don't you feel like having a talk with Leo?"

"What do you mean? I talk to Leo all the time."

"Oh sure," she replied, "but this would be a man-to-man talk. Oh, come on, you know perfectly well what I mean. I'm not going to draw you a picture, you know."

"What about dad?"

Her eyes briefly caught mine. "He's too busy."

My grandfather fulfilled his duty in a scientific manner, to use his term. He explained everything to me in detail. Ludo later benefited from my expertise on the subject. Even so, at the Switchblade a few months back, it was all well and good our knowing everything, but it was getting us nowhere since girls just don't want to hear about it. We finally went our separate ways without having come up with a single bright idea. Ludo was going to pay a prostitute and I was going to keep trying my luck here, there, and everywhere.

That's when dad came back into the picture. He phoned one Friday night in December to let me and my sister know that he'd be meeting us at the corner café at noon the next day, and that he'd be taking us out for lunch. It was brutally cold that particular Saturday, and Miriam, who gets chilled less easily than anyone I know, started making her teeth chatter the minute she spotted dad standing at the bar.

"Everything going okay, kids?" he asked in a strange voice.

My sister groaned that she was freezing, but I just said, "Yeah, everything's fine."

"Great, we're going to a place in the neighborhood," he said, then looked at us out of the corner of his eye. "A lady friend of mine's going to join us there."

Miriam's teeth immediately stopped chattering. "Do we know her, this friend?"

"No, but you'll see, she's very nice."

It gave me a funny feeling to be walking down the street with my dad; it was like he wasn't my father at all, like he was some stranger. For weeks I'd avoided seeing him when he'd ask, but that time I'd given in 'cause I missed him. He still walked that same way, with his shoulders thrown back, but he'd lost his little pot belly, and he was wearing a jacket I'd never seen before. In fact, everything he had on looked brand new. We'd barely sat down at the restaurant when this woman with short red hair and small blue eyes showed up at our table. Dad jumped to his feet.

"José and Miriam, I'd like to introduce you to Erma."

The squinty-eyed redhead spread her thin lips in what was no doubt an attempt at a smile.

"Hi, kids. I've heard so much about you."

Miriam gave the woman her freshest look. "You work in daddy's office?"

"No, Miriam."

"So who are you then?'"

I could tell just by the look on dad's face and I really couldn't get over it. This woman was every bit as sexy as a sack of potatoes.

"I'm your father's companion."

Then *wham*, without missing a beat, my little sister asked, "So what's a companion?"

To create a diversion, dad called over the waitress. I buried my head in the menu. Once she gave up on acting all buddy-buddy with us on account of the faces we were pulling—they must have looked impenetrable—Erma started chatting with her *companion*. I can't remember for the life of me what she said to him. All I know is that my old man was drinking in her words with the stupidest look I've ever seen on his face. Me,

I just went on chewing my steak and wondering if I should tell mom about dad's companion. Miriam would take care of it in any event. I could count on her for that.

After we finished eating, Erma finally turned to us, little blue eyes, scrunched up mouth, and all. "I think you should come back with us to my house. My niece is supposed to meet us there."

My sister slipped her hand into mine and we listlessly climbed into the little Renault belonging to the woman we were to call just plain E from then on. E's pad looked more like a museum than a place where people live. I'd never seen a more spiffed-up apartment in my life. We had barely walked in the door when she asked us to take off our shoes.

In an overly polite tone that hardly boded well, Miriam asked, "What should I do with my sneakers, Madame My-Daddy's-Companion, throw them out the window? I stepped in shit." Then she burst into tears. As dad was trying to comfort her while looking apprehensively at the horrified expression on the museum keeper's face (he gets so jumpy around that lady it makes me wanna puke), the doorbell suddenly rang.

"That must be my niece Sophie," said E, screwing up her face into a smile. Then a brunette with a thick braid down to her waist sauntered up to me.

"You're Luc's son, I suppose?"

Anyway, what with E having disappeared into the far reaches of her museum, Sophie started talking nonstop. She told me that she studied cinema at the National Film Institute and that she'd been depressed ever since her boyfriend cleared out because of some stupid quarrel. Finally she invited me along to see this cute American movie. She hated being in a dark movie theatre alone, she said. Dad and Miriam reappeared at that very moment and, fearing that Sophie might change her mind, I announced that I was going out and that I'd get home on my own. Miriam whined at first, but dad had the presence of mind to promise her a triple-decker ice cream cone, an argument she's rarely able to resist.

So I found myself with my father's companion's niece in a cinema in the Latin Quarter. She was leaning against me all through the movie, and feeling the warmth of her body was making me more and more nervous. Finally, toward the end of the show, she whispered, "I have a room right around the corner. Wanna come over?"

Trembling with excitement, I managed to get out the word *yes*. As soon as the feature ended, I followed her up to her attic room. What comes next I've told Ludo in detail. He maintains, perhaps not without reason, that this girl must have been a nymphomaniac. She pulled off her sweater, revealing a pair of breasts whose nipples were already pointing straight up, then her jeans. I was just standing there.

"C'mon," she said to me in a soft giggle. "Hurry up and get undressed. There's a first time for everything."

Once I was completely naked, she kneeled down

in front of me and licked my dick a few times. Then she lay down on the floor, took my hand, and plunged it into her damp bush.

"Come here," she said in a husky voice.

"But I am here," I replied.

She burst out laughing. "God, you are *so* naïve!" she said as she grabbed me around the waist. "Now come *here*!" And with that she pulled me on top of her. Following several awkward attempts, I finally managed, guided by her fingers, to make my way into something warm and mysterious, then gave a little cry as I ejaculated. Ashamed at having been so gauche, I stammered out, "Excuse me."

She shot me a mocking look and, suddenly feeling vaguely nauseated, I noticed that the skin on her face was coarse and blemished by some lingering acne. The longer I stared, the worse she looked. And then she shoved me off. As I leapt into my clothes, I mumbled that I had to run because my mother would be worried. When at last in my haste I offered her my hand (the idea of kissing her made me sick to my stomach), she practically shrieked. "Get the fuck out of here! I should've just let you die a virgin."

Life is really funny, I said to myself in Paul's peaceful study. If E dropped dead at my feet, it wouldn't be any skin off of my nose; but if it weren't for her, I'd still be a virgin . . .

No one's in the drawing room. Outside, the dogs are howling at the moon, the wind's whistling through the chimney—you'd think you were in the middle of a horror movie. Above my head, a door slams—probably the one to Paul's room. I turn on the TV to lighten up the atmosphere, because ever since Leo said that Jeanne was coming, it hasn't been a lot of fun around here. Everyone's jumpy, myself included.

Just as I'm settling into an easy chair, feet propped up on an ottoman, Billy goes right by without seeing me. "Hey, Billy!" I hiss, but he doesn't stop. Then, after saying something I don't catch, mom shows up. I'm figuring that she'll at least smile at me, but instead, when she sees me, she just sticks her hands into the pockets of her jeans and frowns. In another second she's gonna be screaming 'cause I've turned the TV up too loud.

No, definitely not a lot of fun.

Luc

It was here in this study overlooking the front lawn
with its poplars and its two-hundred-year-old oaks and,
in the distance, the fields of sunflowers and wheat—it
was here that Paul spoke to me for the first time about
the war and the camps. He valued my mind and, since
my parents stubbornly refused to speak of that time,
he probably deemed it his duty to fill me in.

I must have been Miriam's age—she just fell asleep
in the blue bedroom—maybe a year younger, but I remember our conversation as if it were yesterday.

"I was locked up for a long time, my boy. In a
frightful place where they didn't treat people like human beings."

"Why? What had you done?"

"I had been a Resistance fighter. That means I
fought against the Germans who had invaded our
country, and also against certain Frenchmen—those
who were called collaborators because they helped the
enemy."

"But you weren't afraid, Uncle Paul."

He smiled. "Quite the contrary. I always felt fear
in the pit of my stomach, first when I was passing
coded messages to my friends, then when I was taken

prisoner and later transfered to a concentration camp. Fear never gave me a moment's rest."

"And daddy was there with you?"

He looked at me and in his eyes I could make out a certain embarrassment. "No, Luc," he said.

"Where was he then?"

"In Angers splitting time between the hospital and his office. When the war broke out, he had just set up his practice. He was on active duty for a year, then, after the debacle in 1940, he went back home."

"Why wasn't he—what's the word?—a Resistance fighter too?"

Paul took a long drag on the cigar he permitted himself after lunch. "Let's just say that your father and I were not of the same opinion."

His tone was so evasive that I was suddenly gripped by panic. "What did daddy do exactly?"

"Nothing serious, Luc, don't worry about it."

An absolute certainty crept into my mind. My father, this strict, silent man, had acted badly. Later I was to learn that much as he had backed Pétain, he never actively collaborated with the Nazis. But for me, it was over. I was too disappointed to forgive him.

I've often wondered what I would have done in his place. Since I was born in 1945, at the end of the war, I can't say how I would have acted. I suppose that, given my political convictions, I would have sided with the Resistance, but can one ever be sure? My wife and children have tagged me a coward and the word fits me like a glove. Am I? Probably. Not just a coward, but a violent, unpredictable man imbued with bitterness and fascinated like a child by what shines on the outside while remaining blind to what goes on inside myself. These last few years, if I have often failed to keep my word to Sarah by coming home hours late or forgetting plans we'd made in advance, it's been so she could see the real me—someone not good, just like my father. I needed to hear contempt in her voice—such a pretty, affectionate voice at that—to perceive some kind of emotion in the depths of her eyes to go on living, to go on functioning from day to day. I had to make sure that the very person I cared about most in this world was my enemy. Occasionally she would crack and ask me, "Why, Luc, why? You used to be so sweet," and I would brutally reply, "Go on, pull the old teary-eyes trick. Don't mind me!" I couldn't help myself. I couldn't stop playing the horrible game from which I drew my energy. My father, yes, my father again, lost his marbles when my mother died prematurely of cancer. He didn't have anyone to persecute any more. So he set about committing suicide, meticulously, bit by bit.

I open the second drawer of Paul's desk. The little mother-of-pearl revolver is still there. I pick it up and press it to my temple. Will I pull the trigger? Maybe not right away, but soon. What was it Miriam said? That if Erma ordered me to jump out a twelfth-story window, I'd do it. I was happy to be with my loved ones, but when I heard my daughter proclaim her truth, all of a sudden everything crumbled.

The sound of footsteps in the hall makes me jump. "Dad . . . dad?"

José's voice is uncertain. I abruptly realize that I'm still holding the revolver and hastily put it back in its place just before my son pushes open the door to Paul's study.

"Oh, so you're in here? I was wondering where you had gotten off to. Seems like someone's always missing in this dump."

Despite my morbid plans, I can't help smiling. It's definitely the first time I've ever heard anyone call the château a dump. He's looking at me intently, a slight frown on his face. It's exactly the same expression Sarah gets when she's worried about something.

"Well, I wasn't very far away, José. Come in, come in."

He walks toward me, then hesitates before veering over to the settee. He's changed so much in the last six months that I have a hard time recognizing my little boy. I should have made a point of seeing him more often, should have taken an interest in what he was reading, should have gone with him to movies and concerts. He's the easiest child I know to keep entertained. Everything fascinates him. Now I'm wondering how I ever could have deprived myself of the pleasure of seeing him marvel at something new. Erma maintains that he's sullen and that it's quite obvious that his chaotic upbringing has caused him to suffer some kind of mental imbalance. She never says anything at all about Miriam. It's as if she's afraid of that little slip of a nine-year-old girl. But my bright-eyed José is an easy mark. Especially since that episode with her niece. I laughed till I cried when I realized what had happened. That cow Sophie claimed José had practically raped her. But I know that's utterly untrue. She even made a pass at me one weekend when Erma was away visiting family, and I had a hell of a time escaping her clutches myself.

"Dad, have you seen Miriam? Mom's looking for her."

"I left her a good fifteen minutes ago. Don't worry. She won't be going anywhere now. I promised to make her spaghetti carbonara."

"Great, I'm absolutely famished. It's been quite a while since I had some of your spaghetti."

There's a hint of reproach in his voice. When I had the time, I was in charge of family meals. Leo would occupy himself making central European delicacies while I took care of the rest, the important part. It's the same story with Erma. She doesn't think twice about assigning the household chores to me, no doubt figuring I owe her for the material comforts she provides me. But most of all, I loved feeding my children and hearing them shout with admiration that I was the world's best cook.

"What's going on downstairs, José?"

He heaves a heavy sigh. "All hell is breaking loose. Paul's flipping out, Lisa's pouting, and mom's in a bad mood. She wants you to come help her with the cooking."

"Fine, I'll be right down."

He nods his head. I can see by his worried expression that something's bothering him. "Dad, can I ask you a question?"

"Shoot."

"Why'd you agree to have lunch with Jeanne?"

"I didn't *agree*. I invited her."

He stares at me, dumbfounded. He just can't understand that. Much as Sarah, when talking to the children, has always spoken sympathetically of Jeanne, their unknown grandmother, never accusing her of anything, José resents her. He's too warmhearted to accept the idea that a mother could abandon her children.

"Well, I'm off," he says abruptly.

"Tell your mother I'm coming."

"Okay!"

As soon as the door closes, I start thinking about my strange encounter with my mother-in-law. From the first time I met the Abners, I had been fascinated by this story Leo and Lisa never brought up, but which Sarah, on the other hand, spoke of abundantly, on occasion for entire nights at a time. I was receptive then, not closed up the way I am today, and so in love with my wife that I'd try to answer the questions she was forever asking me. She had seen her mother a few years before in Chicago, had found the woman's anguish devastating, and, without directly blaming Leo, had decided that he was responsible for her running away.

One night she asked, "Tell me, Luc, what would you have done in Jeanne's place? Be honest."

"Why, I have absolutely no idea."

"Listen, imagine a perfect man—Leo. His friends admire him. His daughters adore him. He knows how to do everything. He's funny, warm, brave; you get the feeling watching him that he possesses the truth. And then, by contrast, there's this woman whose only asset is being beautiful, but that's not enough. Comparing herself to Leo, she feels small, trivial, useless. So she falls in love with the first man who comes along, a very young man, because at least he admires her. And on a whim she leaves, runs away. Maybe someone had to keep her from going. I was too little to tell her I loved her as much as I loved Leo."

Sarah cried a lot that night. I held her in my arms for a long time, not knowing that one day I would find myself in the same position as Jeanne, and that no one would keep me from going either.

A few weeks ago, Citrus called me at the office. "Hello, Luc. I'm going to give the phone to someone who'd like to talk to you."

Moved by a crazy hope, I told myself: *It's Sarah.* But of course it wasn't. A woman's husky voice, marked by the slightest hint of an accent, was on the other end of the line. "I suppose you have heard about me. I am your wife's mother."

"Jeanne?"

There was a brief pause, then: "Yes, Jeanne. Would you be willing to see me?"

"Of course," I replied unhesitatingly. "We could

have lunch together if you like. Are you free tomorrow?"

The husky voice trembled a little. "Yes. This is very kind of you, Luc, really very kind."

I went to pick her up at Citrus' place, where she was staying. As I shook the hand of this slender woman with her still-beautiful if battered features, I recalled my parents' reaction when they learned that my future mother-in-law had abandoned her husband and daughters. My mother had been on the verge of hysterics. "I'm no anti-Semite, Luc, but these are Israelite goings-on." She was careful never to use the word Jewish. "Those people never stay put."

"But think about their fate over the last two thousand years, mother. They've been driven out everywhere they've gone. The minute they settle somewhere, they're oppressed. You've had it easy being French from way back; you just don't understand."

I knew arguing with her was useless, but her reaction nauseated me. "You'll see," she caustically replied, "that Sarah has you under her spell, but she'll run out on you too."

"Right, and she'll poison the water I drink while she's at it," I screamed before storming out of my parents' house.

Meeting the Abners and living among them, I learned that Judaism wasn't at all what I had imagined. Up until then, I had thought of Jews as sad, bitter people weighed down by their grievous past. But Leo radiated a contagious gaiety. If he worried about his daughters, which was likely the case, he certainly didn't let it show.

At home in their huge, friendly apartment on rue La Bruyère, they all lived from day to day, truly savoring each moment as if unsure that the next day might not bring some disastrous calamity. Even being driven into exile was a favorite topic for jokes. One day, after a particularly strong showing by the extreme right in France, I was rather shocked to hear Sarah screaming with laughter as she talked on the phone with one of her girlfriends, also a Jew. "We'll have to make sure we get sent to the same camp," she said.

When I gaped at her, she shot back, "Don't look at me like that, Luc. If I can't joke about all these horrors, I might as well kill myself right now."

But subsequently I learned of her many anxieties, principal among them being her utter panic at the prospect of taking a trip. José was about a year old, and we had decided to spend a few days in Venice. She seemed happy at the idea of going, but when I came home the day before we were to leave, I found her standing like a statue in front of her clothes closet, her face streaked with tears.

"What's wrong, Sarah? Bad news? Speak to me."

Wringing her hands, she replied. "The bad news is that I can't pack my suitcase. I'd rather stay here."

"I'm going to help you. Just calm down. What is it exactly that you're afraid of?"

BÉATRICE SHALIT

"Of leaving, of finding nothing when I come back—oh, I don't know!"

At the time, I didn't understand at all, but Lisa, who suffers from the same malady—her big sister packs her bags whenever she goes to one of her conferences—Lisa calmly explained it to me. "I think it has something to do with the camps. We make jokes about them, but they've affected us, all the more so because Sarah and I were born after the war."

I agreed but thought to myself that, perhaps unconsciously, she was concealing part of the truth from me, that if both of them were so afraid of going away, it was because Jeanne had left before them and never come back.

Now the mystery woman was there before me, her eyes the same golden hue as Sarah's.

"Shall we go?" I asked.

"Yes, I am ready."

I took Jeanne to a Chinese restaurant in the twentieth. We talked about Leo's illness, her life in Chicago, and especially about Miriam, whom she had often picked up secretly at school since her return to France.

"That little one is always so quick with an answer. Sarah was a bit like that as a child. She would tell me stories to keep me entertained at night. I adored her, you know. Has she changed?"

I found Jeanne's naïve question moving. "I didn't know her as a child," I replied, "but she still has as lively an imagination as ever."

At the end of the meal, she asked me rather brutally, "Why did you invite me to lunch? Out of pity?"

I hesitated at first. "No," I murmured. "Because I'm like you. I too have left, and I don't know how to return."

She laid a hand on my arm. "You must not wait too long. Otherwise, your life will be over, your children will have forgotten you, and it will be too late."

Sarah

"Mommy, daddy's unhappy."

Chaos reigns in the kitchen, which has gradually been filling up with the better part of the château's guests. Because I'm busy washing greens for the salad, I don't notice Miriam come in. She has gotten up on tiptoe and pressed her mouth to my ear. Surprised, I turn to her so suddenly that several lettuce leaves fall at my feet.

Her eyes are fixed on mine and their expression is solemn, almost accusatory. "Did you hear me?" she whispers.

"Yes."

"So what are you going to do?"

Hugging her to me, I murmur into her hair. "Listen, Miriam, we can't talk here right now."

"Then when?"

"In a few minutes, as soon as I've finished making the salad dressing. Okay?"

Head held to one side, she hesitates. She would like me to drop everything and follow her. Patience is not one of her virtues.

"Well, okay," she ends up saying halfheartedly.

My gaze follows her. She sits down on the bench

where Lisa and I were sitting and watches me, arms folded determinedly. Her blue nightshirt, on which gleam silvery letters spelling out the slogan DOWN WITH APARTHEID, covers her padded slippers.

Once a month, on an afternoon when Miriam doesn't have school, Leo comes to pick up his granddaughter and take her clothes shopping. The results of their expeditions are breathtaking. They both adore anything out of the ordinary, and it makes little difference to them that what they delightedly bring back at night is perfectly unwearable. Once their booty is arrayed on the couch, Leo separates out the sweatshirts and a few other items that one of his old friends then imprints with slogans. The one adorning the blue nightshirt figures among the tamer of the lot. My father's fanciful initiatives no longer surprise me. They really rather make me smile instead—but when Luc would come home at night after one of these expeditions and find Miriam in front of the bathroom mirror strutting about in her new clothes, he would take me aside and beg me to explain to my father once and for all that our daughter was not a walking billboard, and that she didn't work in a circus.

I, however, find the gaudy bad taste of those garments moving, probably because it reminds me of the time when Leo used to dress my sister and me. Even as a little girl, Lisa would stand firm and say no to all that my father suggested. I, on the other hand, went to even greater extremes of flashiness and mismatching of colors, my principal goal having always been to attract attention . . .

Leo is sitting a few feet away from me, flask in hand, talking with Billy. I hear him proclaim that having memories may not be essential to life. And what would I do without memories? I'd cease to exist, I'd dissolve into nothingness.

"Mommy, are you coming?"

"Wait a minute. You can see perfectly well I haven't finished yet."

She's pouting now. The truth of the matter is that I have no desire to know that Luc is unhappy. Another woman has taken responsibility for him, for his moods and comfort, and she is no doubt doing a much better job of it than I ever did. Sometimes I see E, whom I've never met, in my dreams. Strangely enough, she always appears to me dressed in a uniform. If I'm in a generous mood, she's dressed like a meter maid or a nurse. Otherwise she generally wears the striped pajamas of a convict.

When Luc started living with her, I thought I'd go mad with jealousy. Each time the children would come back from their Sunday lunch with her and Luc, I couldn't help interrogating them. "What was Erma wearing? What did she talk about at the restaurant? What did she order? Was dad nice to her?" The questions seemed innocuous enough, but I would rain them down in such an anxious tone that they would both just stare at me in amazement. I practically choked with rage the day José innocently told me about E's latest exploit. "You know, mom, Erma went to some kind of camp to quit smoking and it worked. You're going to kill yourself if you keep going at your rate. Maybe you should try it too." Poor kids. Not only was I neglecting them, but their prudent refusal to say much was driving me up the wall.

In my delirium, I was prey to several obsessions about Luc and E. First of all, I was constantly imagining their erotic endeavors, but always absurdly exaggerated to avoid causing myself pain. He entered her through every possible orifice, even her ears on occasion. She swallowed his sperm with delight, then smeared it on her face because it was good for her assuredly waxy complexion. She whinnied like a horse when she came, or pretended to come, while Luc groaned with pleasure.

Perhaps in reaction to my sister's amorous excesses, I have always treated all that relates to sex with disdain, as if it were a domain that didn't concern me. Even my novels are oppressively prudish. Despite the remarkable patience Luc demonstrated, in his arms I was as passionate as an ironing board. As soon as he'd start fondling me with desire, I'd babble at a dizzying speed about this, that, and the other thing. Sometimes I'd tell funny stories—hardly the accompaniment most favorable to erotic excitement. Sometimes I'd just recount what had happened to me during the day. Making love with him felt like some sort of incestuous act. I was probably too young and inexperienced when I met him. I thought he was attractive, I liked touching his smooth skin. But he didn't turn me on.

Then there was another obsession I spent a solid month brooding over in deadly earnest: coming up with schemes for assassinating my rival. I could wait for her outside the office where she lavished advice on couples having trouble—how awful—then plant a kitchen knife right in her heart. Assuming she had a heart—it wasn't clear. Or perhaps, more discreet if less gratifying, I could hire a contract killer. Obviously I was losing my mind.

One morning at roughly that point in time, I received a little note from the stand-up comedian. He had suffered a stroke a few months earlier and no longer went out. "It seems you have troubles, Sarah. Come visit me. I'll be waiting." I had no desire to discuss the troubles in question, but out of friendship for him, I visited that very day.

He and his wife had moved to a posh suburb. She answered the door. "Here you are at last, my dear! Our funny man is being absolutely impossible. He claims he'd rather cut his throat than go on vegetating like a zucchini. If only you could cheer him up. He adores you, you know."

I promised to try and make my old accomplice see reason, knowing full well the futility of the task. To the best of my knowledge, no one had ever succeeded in making the comedian see reason. Knocking first, I entered his bedroom. Sitting motionless in an armchair, eyes unfocused, he looked a painful sight.

"Master, I'm here."

He turned his head with difficulty. "Oh, it's you, Zoro, you've come."

I called him Master from the beginning and he dubbed me Zoro after the title of the first routine I ever wrote for him.

"So, Master, when exactly are you committing suicide?"

"Don't you start hounding me too, my pretty."

"Because we could do it together, if you like."

He gave a slight chuckle. "So tell me, Sarah. I hear you aren't doing so well yourself."

"No, I'm not."

"Your father says you spend your days wandering around looking gloomy."

I sighed. "It's because of Luc."

"Zoro, you're quite a character. First you chuck that boy out the door, which wasn't very astute of you to begin with, seeing as he has tremendous virtues, principal among them his ability to abide you. And now you're moping! Isn't that it?"

I could hear his wife bustling about in the next room. Perhaps she was listening at the door. "Do you find me as awful as all that?" I whispered.

"Let's just say you're no prize. Are you writing at least?"

"No, not a word."

With great difficulty, he reached out a hand to me. "Come closer. The two of us made quite a team, eh? You can talk to me, you know."

"I don't want to talk." A single tear rolled down my cheek to the end of my nose."

"Listen, Sarah, let yourself go. Share some of your troubles with your old partner."

"I'm so confused," I murmured, slipping my hand into his. "If you only knew! He's found himself another woman."

"Better a woman than a man."

"Don't make me laugh."

"Okay, okay. Some trollop who wears skirts that barely cover her behind?"

"No, worse. A middle-aged matron who's loaded to boot. She brings him along everywhere—concerts, fancy dinner parties, premieres . . . everywhere. He used to die of boredom at plays, but she gets him to go to four-hour Claudel monstrosities. Anyway, you get the idea, a real culture vulture. And now monsieur has gone and spent three weeks in Peru with that creature. When he was living at home, he never had time for anything."

"But Zoro, you *hate* leaving your nest, and you faint at the mere mention of a trip. So have you met this woman?"

"No, thank God, but I despise her. What's more, her name is Erma. Erma! Can you believe it?"

"And what does this Erma do in life?"

"She's a marriage counselor."

He broke out in his husky laugh, and I had to bite my lips to keep from laughing myself. "You could go see her about patching up your differences with Luc.

However the session went, it would make one hell of a routine."

"Don't think it hasn't crossed my mind. Oh, Master, what do you think I should do? I haven't admitted it to anyone, but I miss Luc."

He threw his head back. "Hmmm. You see each other from time to time?"

"No, never. We talk on the telephone."

"And are you nice at least?"

"Awful. Hardly two seconds go by and already I'm screaming at him—I can't control myself."

"Listen, kid, that's not the way it's done. How about using a little common sense? He's found himself another woman, but that doesn't mean he's forgotten you. I'm no marriage counselor myself, but I say make him laugh, be sweet, and flirt a little!"

I flashed a weak smile. "I suppose you're right. Anyway, I'll let you know how I'm doing. So what about you? You're not going to keep harping on this suicide nonsense, are you?"

He gave me his darkest look. "Yes, I am. I'm old, and I have every right to complain. But don't worry, I'll let you know when I make up my mind. Will you come back and see me again sometime, Zoro? I was a success before, eh? I miss it, you know."

I deposited a kiss on his withered cheek. "I know. But you were the best. Nobody ever had as many enemies as you." Running down the list of his enemies was one of the comedian's favorite amusements.

"Thank you, Zoro," he replied. "I really get a kick out of you."

The visit bucked up my spirits. In fact, I then went through a rather peaceful period—before confronting first José's drug story and then Leo's illness . . .

The noise has grown more intense in the kitchen of the château. "Sarah, your daughter's calling you. You must've been washing those same greens for a full fifteen minutes. What have you been thinking about?"

"Nothing special, Leo. My mind was elsewhere, that's all."

Not far from me, Luc is bustling about with his usual energy. He's rolled up the sleeves of his sweatshirt and tied a dishrag around his waist by way of an apron. Miriam is tugging at my sleeve.

"Mommy, you're not being nice. You think it's fun waiting for you?"

"I'm coming, my darling."

She's dragging me all the way upstairs in the direction of Paul's study.

"We don't need to go this far, Miriam. Nobody can hear us from here."

"Yes we do, mommy. I want to show you something."

"What?"

"You'll see," she whispers.

She tiptoes up to the study door, a conspiratorial look on her face, then pushes it open. "You know this place well, mommy?"

"Yes, I come here often. Why?"

"Just now, as I was walking out of the blue bedroom, I went up here because I heard footsteps. The door wasn't shut all the way." She stops talking and looks at me, eyes wide with fear.

Suddenly worried, I ask her, "And then?"

"Daddy was sitting there, behind the desk. He opened a drawer. I'm going to show you what he did."

She opens the second drawer from the top and, to my horror, takes out a revolver which she then presses to her temple. "Miriam," I scream, dashing toward her, "put that down right now." But she has already laid the revolver on the desk.

"Mommy, do you think he wanted to shoot?"

"No, no, of course not. What an idea!"

Crying frantically, she jumps into my arms. "It's my fault, mommy. I wasn't nice to him."

"Calm down, my dear. It can't be your fault."

"Yes, it can. I was mean to him on purpose when he came to see me in the blue bedroom."

"Did you tell him things you didn't think were true?"

"No, I told him the truth. But I knew he wouldn't get mad 'cause I had just fallen in the stream."

Running short of arguments, I stroke her cheek. "What do you want me to do, Miriam?"

"I want you to talk to him. I don't want my daddy to die like Leo."

"But Leo's still alive, dear. Tell me, have you talked with José about what you saw?"

She shakes her head vigorously. "No. So are you going to talk to daddy?"

"Yes, that's a promise. Shall we go back down?" I ask, but she clings to me, preventing me from moving.

"Mommy, are you happy to be seeing Jeanne again?"

"Yes, of course."

"You're not ever going to leave me, are you mommy?"

"No, no, of course not. Never ever."

"Because if Leo's gone and daddy's gone, then you'll be the only one I have left."

"Don't worry, darling. Come on, let's get a move on. It's time for dinner."

On the second-floor landing we run into Paul coming out of his bedroom. "Sarah," he says to me, "I shouldn't have snapped at you. I do apologize. But I've aged ten years since the lot of you got here. You're not going to frighten me any more, are you, little Miriam?"

"No, Uncle Paul. I'm too hungry."

As he's walking down the stairs with a heavy tread, my daughter and I exchange glances, united by our secret. All of a sudden I'm terribly worried. I have a hard time imagining Luc blowing his brains out, but who knows? All those people he used to win over with his charm and vigor never would have imagined just how somber and withdrawn he can become. Seeing him in his armchair sitting motionless behind a newspaper, I've often suspected he was mulling over dark thoughts

the same way his unfortunate father did. But the minute I'd ask the slightest question, he'd fly off the handle. "Don't you have anything better to do than bother
me?" he'd shout. "If you worked all day like everybody else, you'd understand why I'm beat." Faced with
his aggressiveness, I could do nothing but keep quiet.
Now I'm going to have to sound him out tactfully,
and tact is hardly my strong suit.

"Sarah?" I hear my father's resounding voice near me.
"Yes?"

"You look worried, treasure. Want me to tell you
a funny story?"

"Oh please, Leo, not right now."

José

In the kitchen they're all swilling down white wine and looking chipper, which is certainly a nice change from the heavy-duty frowns they were pulling before. After checking out that scene, I go back into the drawing room and sprawl in that easy chair across from the TV. I'm busy flipping channels—there's nothing to really sink your teeth into on Saturday night—when I feel a hand muss my hair and practically jump so high I hit the ceiling.

"Did I scare you?"

"Oh, it's you, Paul. Feeling better?"

He sighs. "I'm trying to live from moment to moment and stop thinking about what might yet happen, kid. You know, José, you are the least convincing junkie I've ever seen."

"So you've been hanging out with the real thing?"

"No, not really."

"Maybe you should start broadening your personal horizons."

He breaks out his ringing laugh. "Truly, José, my current horizons are broad enough to provide me with adequate stimulation. Tell me something: you like Adeline, don't you."

I try not to blush. "Oh . . ."

"Come now, it was obvious the way you were sizing her up. Don't tell her I said so, but in the end she may not have been wrong to back out of her marriage."

"What's her fiancé like?"

"Dull, I must admit."

At that point, after glancing toward the kitchen, where a crescendo of voices is rising, he pulls up another easy chair and sits down next to me. I can tell he wants to talk about what's been going on.

"Leo looks like he's feeling better. If I didn't know about the seriousness of his condition, I'd even say he was fit as a fiddle. Your mother told me he's the one who amuses himself having all kinds of slogans put on Miriam's clothes. When I read the inscription lettered on her nightshirt, I was rather surprised to see she was so politically aware at her age."

"You haven't seen the sweats I wear to school, Uncle Paul. They've got all sorts of funny things written on them."

My sister has materialized between us like some little demon. I go, "Miriam, couldn't you let us talk in peace for once? You're always sticking your nose into stuff that's none of your business."

"You're such a drag, José," she replies as she hops into Paul's lap.

"Tell me, doll," says Paul, "do you know what apartheid is?"

"Okay, in South Africa there's this regime run by

a bunch"—Paul listens in amazement. "A regime?" he interrupts.

I want to start laughing because I know what's coming next.

"A regime run by a bunch of bananas," Miriam declares.

Our host smiles at me over her head. "Well, she certainly is quite politically aware, I must say."

She gives both of us an annoyed look. "Fine then. I'm gonna go tell grandpa the joke about Toto. At least *he* doesn't make fun of me."

Once she's run off, Paul gets up and pours himself a glass of port. "I need a pick-me-up after all the agitation I've endured," he mutters.

"And it's not over yet," I remark softly.

"No, it's not."

He sits back down, looking pensive, glass of port in hand. Then he bends toward me and asks in a confidential undertone, "Just between you and me, kid, do you think Leo's capable of getting Citrus to help him invent this entire cancer business out of whole cloth?"

He's taken his time about getting to the point, but I'm hardly surprised because I'd had exactly the same thought. I put on my most laid-back expression. "Of course he's capable of it. But why would he? There's no real reason."

He rubs his chin. "Oh, but there is, and it makes perfect sense—to bring Jeanne back. Come on, José, you're nobody's fool. Hasn't that thought crossed your mind?"

I shrug my shoulders. "Vaguely. But there's one detail that doesn't fit. Why should it be so difficult to get Jeanne back? She mad at him or what?"

"That I can't tell you, kid."

There's something in his voice that intrigues me, so I press on. "Well, you certainly must be in on the whole story, knowing both of them the way you do."

He sighs. "It's such an old story. Has Leo confided any of it to you?"

"Yes, but only a little, this very afternoon in the ghost room as a matter of fact. He told me she had fallen in love with another man."

Paul looks at me. "I see," he says. "I admire your grandfather a great deal, you know. But when he met Jeanne, he was going through a rather confused period in his life. He was seething with excitement, wanted to do everything at once; he couldn't sit still. The minute he saw a woman, he fell in love with her. Do you understand my meaning, José?"

"She left because . . ." I'm so shocked I can't even bring myself to go on.

"Yes," Paul murmurs, "exactly. That time it was some nightclub singer—a blonde with a screechy voice who was always dreadfully over-madeup. By pure chance I ran into them one night at a restaurant in Montparnasse."

I suddenly feel a bitter taste building up in my mouth. I'm mad at Paul for destroying my illusions. And to think I took my grandfather for a saint! I feel like I just went crashing down a staircase headfirst. I couldn't care less if dad goes and leers at every chick he sees—he's never been shy on that front, not even when mom's around—but that Leo should be capable of the same or worse, *that* blows me away.

"José? José, have I upset you? Listen, I've handled this badly. You mustn't blame your grandfather. Jeanne was a strange woman. I could never tell if she was passive or stoic. She'd have only had to say the word, and Leo would have stopped chasing after every woman he saw. He was provoking her, you understand. But she kept still."

"She had a . . . well, a someone, herself?"

"A very young man who was completely overwhelmed by her beauty. She consoled herself as best she could. I never should have told you all this; I can see you're upset by the look in your eyes."

"No, that's okay," I reply softly. "I'm going for a little fresh air before dinner."

The weather outside is mild. Raindrops are sliding down my forehead, but I can breathe better than I could in the drawing room. As I'm walking, I think about some words Leo said to me just two years ago. "Men can't always act like heroes, José. Don't judge your father too harshly. He's muddling through as best he can. I've often acted badly myself." Maybe he was refering to the whole business with Jeanne, but in the end I just don't know.

This talk happened at the time when my father really started screwing around. It seemed like his job, the so-called VIPs he was seeing, and the cocktail parties thrown by some clown or other were all going to his head. The three of us didn't count for beans. This guy who used to spend so much time taking care of me no longer even knew exactly which grade I was in or what courses I was taking. Mom would yell at us over the tiniest little detail. Basically, life was a mess.

And right in the middle of all that, it got worse. One afternoon the headmistress of Miriam's school called the house. "Please don't panic, madame, but Miriam has gone and done something very stupid."

"Is she alive, at least?"

"Of course, of course. What a thing to say. Only she ate some corn laced with rat poison."

Hearing that, mom threw on the first jacket she could lay her hands on and called my father at the office. When a secretary answered and told her that he was in a meeting and couldn't be disturbed, she told me herself that she shot right back with "Oh, by all means don't disturb his meeting. Just tell him that his daughter has been in a terrible accident."

Then she hung up the phone so violently that she tore it off the wall. She ran all the way to Miriam's school, where a fire truck and an ambulance were parked out front. Through the window, she could make out a bunch of little girls gathered in the inner courtyard. Among them was Miriam, who turned and gave her a trembly smile.

"The paramedic just called the poison control center," the headmistress explained. "He's waiting to hear back. And to think it was a little girl six years old who had that corn in her pocket. I have no idea where she found it. Anyway, she offered it around in the bathroom. I'm surprised your Miriam was involved. She's usually so sensible."

After a long consultation between the paramedic and the poison control center, it was decided that the little girls should be sent to the hospital to have their stomachs pumped.

"And they'll be out of danger after that?" asked mom, trying with all her might not to cry.

"Maybe. But there's still a risk of cerebral hemorrhaging."

On that less than reassuring note, my mother ran home to pack an overnight bag containing two dolls and a nightshirt. She also left a message for me: *Don't worry, my José. I'm with your sister at Trousseau Hospital, but she's doing fine. Take a taxi and meet us there if you like.*

I had come home from school with Ludo that day. Sometimes we do our homework together. He was the one who found the note on my desk. I was in the kitchen pouring us two glasses of Coke when he came over to me.

"Hey, José, take a look at this," he said in a lifeless voice.

Surprised by his tone, I shot back, "What, something wrong?"

"Not with me. It's your sister. Look."

After reading the note, I was paralyzed with fear at

the thought of God knows what, but Ludo snapped me out of it. "Come on, don't get all worked up. Just step on it. I'll help you find a cab."

At the hospital, they sent me to the emergency room. I found my sister lying on a stretcher with an IV sticking out of her left arm. She was crying as she clung to mom's hand. Mom was flushed bright red herself.

"What happened to you, Miriam?"

A nurse explained the whole business about the corn and the rat poison to me.

"That sure was clever. But why does she have all those red blotches on her face, and how come her eyes are bloodshot?"

"It's a reaction to having her stomach pumped."

"Is she going to have to stay here for long?"

"Just two days, José," my mother finally said. "Everything's going to be all right now."

"And where's dad?"

Silence.

"Well, answer me!"

She bit her lower lip. "In a meeting."

"What did you say? In a *meeting*! No, I must be dreaming."

I raced like a madman back up to the main floor and down the hallway. As I neared the glass doors, I ran into someone.

"Hey, José, stop! Stop already!"

It was my father.

"What happened to her?" he shouted.

I have absolutely no idea what came over me. Whenever I think about it, I feel ashamed. "She's dead," I replied.

He looked at me, then put a hand to his forehead and started shaking from head to toe.

"Dad!"

He couldn't hear me. I tugged at the sleeve of his jacket. "Dad!" I repeated.

"Huh?" His brown eyes had gone glassy.

"It's not true. She's waiting for you downstairs in the emergency room. She'll be out of the hospital day after tomorrow."

"But . . . then why . . . why did you say that to me?" His voice was barely audible.

"Because you weren't there. Again."

He regained his composure with breathtaking speed, and by the time he appeared before mom and Miriam, he had his everyday expression back, that of a guy who's overworked. *Too bad,* I thought. *Maybe he should have let them see that he was scared to death.*

He stayed for ten minutes, just long enough to take care of the admittance forms, then said, "I've got to get back to the office."

"Are you going to come visit me, daddy?" Miriam, who's normally so detached, was eyeing him intently.

"Yes, my darling, tomorrow."

"When tomorrow?"

"Let's say noon. Okay?"

After he kissed her, he did something so thoughtless I'm going to remember it for the rest of my life.

He pulled out his day-planner and said out loud as he was writing: "Hospital. Miriam." That's when I realized my father was two men at the same time: the one I had seen fifteen minutes before who would tear his eyes out to save us from any danger and another I didn't know who was capable of writing *Hospital. Miriam* in his day-planner. Was he play-acting? I don't think so.

Leo came around suppertime, arms full of packages for my sister.

"You really shouldn't have," mom protested. "She did something awfully dumb, you know."

"She won't do it again," countered my grandfather. "Will you, pussycat?"

A few days later, unable to keep it in any longer, I told Leo about my father's weird behavior. That's when he came out with that business about not always being able to act like a hero.

"Your father works hard. He'd like all of you to be proud of him. You have to show him a little more understanding."

"Why doesn't he stop knocking himself out like that if it drives him half crazy? We don't give a damn about the money. He could stay home all day and cook—and we'd just tighten our belts a little."

Leo gave me his most piercing look. "He's arranged his life differently, José. I think it's too late."

Too late, yes, it's all too late. I'll never know who my father really is. I've come to the end of the driveway without realizing it.

"José, dinner's ready," someone says near me.

I hastily turn around and recognize the amnesiac.

"Come on, let's get moving. Your father has made a big platter of spaghetti."

My father is standing on the front porch with a wooden spoon in his hand. "I was starting to worry about you, José."

He's using that sweet, warm voice of his that always makes me lose it. It's all well and good for me to swear I won't get fooled again, but every time I hear that voice, I jump to it just the same.

"I needed to get a little fresh air."

"Yes, I understand," he says, and after letting Billy go inside first, the two of us enter the château together.

Luc

It was in the vicinity of the château d'Amboise, during a weekend we spent with a friend of mine who owned a house on the banks of the Loire, that I opened one of Sarah's notebooks for the first time. I was intrigued by the contents of those notebooks she so abundantly consumed. She bought a new one roughly once a month, even slipping it under her pillow before falling asleep in case she came up with a gag for her wretched boss in the middle of the night. We were just starting our life together, and I never would have dreamed of being so indiscreet if my wife's behavior during those two mid-October days hadn't struck me as strange—in fact, paranoid.

When I enthusiastically informed her of the invitation extended by my high school friend, she gave me a hostile look. Since I was madly in love with her at the time, she had only to bat her eyelashes, and I would tremble at the idea of displeasing her in any way.

"What's wrong, Sarah?"

"Nothing. Only that area is full of châteaux. And if you persist in dragging me about to see all those old stones, I'm warning you: I'll simply die of boredom."

"First of all," I patiently replied, "I'm not going

to *drag* you anywhere. Furthermore, it's magnificent around there, especially in the fall. Flaubert himself was amazed when he toured the château d'Amboise. He wrote somewhere that the Loire is the most French of French rivers."

"Mmmm, that's just it!"

"What's just what?"

Her eyes, now icy, settled on me as she sighed half-heartedly. "No, nothing. You wouldn't understand."

Oh, I understood all right. I might have been a newcomer, a raw freshman in the post-graduate school of Abner family life, but I had already learned that for them, the word *French* had clearly negative connotations. Perhaps I had found favor in Sarah's eyes because of my part Mongolian ancestry. Sensing her initial reservations about me, I had talked at length about it. I'd also recounted to her the story of my great-uncle Henri, a man to whom I apparently bore an uncanny resemblance. A distinguished graduate of the renowned Polytechnical Institute, at the age of forty he permanently took to his bed and surrounded himself with books. She had liked that anecdote. "Quite the Slav, that great-uncle of yours," she had said, flashing me an indulgent smile.

But to get back to that long-ago weekend . . . the night before we were to leave for my friend's house, she asked me, "What does he do, this Eric?"

"Patrick. He works for an ad agency. I think he's in marketing."

"Marketing!"

From her horrified expression, you would have thought I had just announced that my school chum was an executioner, or something close to it. Muzzled by my passion for her, I refrained from mentioning certain people who worked as mercenaries for a tasteless comedian who would remain nameless. (I must admit that when I first learned my shy, timid Sarah was responsible for the fearsome "Zoro"—a routine that is certainly very funny but also devastatingly cruel—I had really thought she suffered from a split personality.)

"You'll see. Patrick's a decent guy—and funny too, even if he's *not* telling Jewish jokes every two seconds."

"That would be the last straw. There's nothing worse than goys trying to tell Jewish jokes. Who else will be there?"

"I have no idea."

She raised her eyebrows in a gesture of utter disbelief. "What! You mean you didn't find out?"

Unable to control myself any longer, I finally exploded. "Oh come on, Sarah, are you looking to pick a fight or what? If you're going to take this attitude, I'm going to cancel the whole trip."

She sighed. "Don't be angry. I just thought you knew me better than that. When I go somewhere, I need to know exactly who I might run up against."

Stunned, I recalled the many friends, friends of friends, casual acquaintances, and unknown cousins from Israel, America, or Australia who were constantly passing through the Abner home on rue La Bruyère. But of course those people weren't French.

"So you need a detailed guest list?" I asked, doing my best to adopt a neutral tone.

"Try to understand me, Luc. I'm completely paralyzed in front of strangers."

As I stared at her, I was thinking that for her, anyone who wasn't part of the Diaspora was a stranger. But faced with her tearful look, I ended up giving in.

"Okay, I'll go call Patrick."

She gazed at me in silence, then stroked my cheek, no doubt moved by my goodwill. "You feel uncomfortable about phoning him back?"

"A little, Sarah."

"Oh, forget it then. As long as you promise to protect me."

Relieved, I embraced her tenderly, just as she muttered under her breath, "Marketing, for Chrissake!"

Thinking back on that disastrous weekend, I realize it was then that our first rift developed.

We left early Saturday morning. To give her a chance to see more of the countryside, I decided to take back roads. About forty miles from Paris, she suddenly said in a choked voice, "Luc, I've forgotten my hair dryer."

"But Sarah, your hair is magnificent."

"Not when it's dirty."

I slowed down slightly. "Fine. You want us to go back and get it?"

Pause.

"No, no, I'll put my hair up in a bun. It'll make my head look like a pear, and those strangers will think I'm hideous, that's all."

As I muttered, "You're exaggerating," I suddenly wondered if I wouldn't have been better advised to call the whole thing off. Then, as we were driving through groves of trees whose autumn-tinted leaves reflected in her eyes, she lit a cigarette and started telling me what had happened in the latest book she had read, an American novel whose title I've forgotten but whose subject I recall clearly: the break-up of a marriage. Alas, I should have had my guard up, but instead, I dropped my defenses and listened, spellbound.

As Sarah herself would be the first to admit, she is anything but a scenery hound. Tourist attractions leave her cold. She does, however, possess a remarkable talent for storytelling. I don't know anyone else who's as good at fleshing out characters or settings in a few sentences, and sometimes with just one or two well-chosen words. For me, it was sensual pleasure to hear her voice choke with laughter as she hit upon the sharpest, funniest adjective or the most expressive metaphor.

She once confided to me at the beginning of our relationship: "If I couldn't tell you what I notice every day—those observations I turn into anecdotes—I would be very unhappy."

"But I love listening to you, Sarah," I had replied with the greatest sincerity.

To make a long story short, we arrived at Patrick's

place around lunchtime. Five or six people were sitting next to the fireplace in a semicircle. As I shook hands all around, I tossed out a few admiring remarks about the house—a disgusting habit of mine according to Sarah. ("And that sickeningly jovial tone of yours is enough to make a person vomit.") She was standing alone at the other end of the room, fidgeting like a nervous little girl.

"Are you coming, Sarah? I want to introduce you to Patrick and his friends."

"Luc," she whispered, giving me a desperate look, "I have to talk to you."

Sensing disaster, I turned to her. "What is it?"

"I'm allergic to smoke."

"Listen, we're going to be sitting down to lunch soon. You'll be far from the fireplace. Don't you want to say hello?"

She promptly obeyed, greeting the group collectively without looking at anyone, tears spilling from her eyes.

By an unfortunate coincidence, all but one of Patrick's other guests worked for the same advertising agency he did, the only exception being a girl studying literature who introduced herself as a poetess. When I saw the look on Sarah's face as the girl told her "The two of us are on the same side," I finally realized that our weekend in the Loire Valley was destined to end in utter disaster.

For most of the meal, Sarah sat there with her jaws firmly clenched. Recalling that memorable lunch in my parents' house, I anxiously looked on as she downed impressive quantities of red wine. When a plate laden with cheese was brought out, the conversation shifted to the relative merits of various kinds of chèvre. Having learned the hard way that Sarah can't abide food talk for more than three seconds, I was wracking my brain trying to come up with some other topic when one of the ad men, a guy who spoke in a loud, pompous voice, made this remark: "I'm no chauvinist, far from it, but in truth, the French are the only people with a proper appreciation for cheese."

I looked cautiously in Sarah's direction. Seated quite far from me at the other end of the table, she was contemplating the contents of her plate with a falsely puzzled look that hardly boded well. Making her first utterance since our arrival, she said in a syrupy voice to the fellow who had just spoken, "Unfortunately for my father, he is Russian by birth. I'm sorry to have to inform you that he is Jewish as well. Do you know what he ate in his concentration camp while your parents were tranquilly sampling their two hundred seventy-three varieties of cheese before conceiving a good little patriot like you? Cat got your tongue? Here, maybe this will loosen it."

Then, as she favored him with an angelic smile, she tossed her glass of wine right in his face. A shudder of amazement ran through all of us. Unsure whether to start laughing hysterically or die of embarrassment, I grabbed Sarah by the shoulders and led her upstairs to the bedroom Patrick had prepared for us.

Before falling asleep—the wine had knocked her out—she murmured, "Anti-Semites, every one. Never mention sales and marketing—or cheese—to me ever again. I feel like throwing myself in the Loire."

That night, while she obstinately turned her back to me in her sleep, I opened her notebook, fully expecting to find a litany of complaints. But instead, under the date October 15, I read:

Luc gone this afternoon with that awful band of reactionaries to tour the château d' Amboise. Fell back asleep and dreamed of the poetess. Rework the bit about cheese and the French. It'll make a great routine. The Master could do a wonderful imitation of that self-satisfied creep's voice—I sure put him in his place. I really am deeply indebted to Luc for bringing me here. If it weren't for him, I'd never have known such people existed. Edifying glimpse of the real France. If a guy like Hitler appeared today, they'd be capable of gassing the lot of us for not properly appreciating their wines and cheeses.

From then on, every time Sarah seemed sullen or sad, I'd take a look at her notebook to find out if she was really in a bad mood or just pretending. But as the situation between us grew steadily worse, instead of talking to her directly—that would have been normal, but I've never known how to do it—I would read her notebook almost daily, seeking to understand through her notes and dreams who she really was, and who I really was as well. For in Sarah's notebooks I would discover my own doubts and insecurities. The minute she described me tenderly, I would melt and become the sweetest of men, but when she started being afraid of me, dreaming once, for example, that I wanted to murder her, I would grow cruel, conforming to the image of me reflected in her writings . . .

"Luc! Luc! What's with you?"

"Huh? Oh, nothing. My mind was just elsewhere."

She looks at me, fork in hand. Between mouthfuls of spaghetti, Paul and Leo are having a heated political discussion. Adeline and Billy are joking around with the children, but Lisa, seated next to her sister, looks kind of tense.

"What were you thinking about, Luc?"

In my wife's luminous eyes, I seem to make out a glimmer of anxiety.

"You mean you're interested?" My voice is too rough. With Sarah, I'm always on the defensive.

No doubt afraid that another argument is about to break out between us, Paul has just looked up.

"Yes, I am," she replies. "Well?"

Suddenly taken aback by the gentleness in her tone, I say, "I was thinking about a cheese platter."

She smiles. "I really outdid myself that day."

Looking at each of us in turn somewhat apprehensively, José asks, "What'd ya do, mom?"

"Oh, I was very impolite to some friends of your

father's. But he forgave me a few days later when I informed him that I was pregnant with you."

She was never more radiant than when she was expecting José. After two months of nausea, she woke me up one night to request cheese—*French* cheese. "All two hundred seventy-three varieties," she specified. I bought out this fancy twenty-four-hour place to make her happy, and we cried with laughter as we stayed up until six in the morning sampling our cheese.

"Luc, buddy, your spaghetti was treating."

The amnesiac is calling me his *buddy* now. I respond with a somewhat curt thank-you.

Miriam corrects the amnesiac. "You don't say *treating*, Billy. You say *delicious* or *tasty*."

She's sitting on my lap. After putting her little hand on the hollow of my neck, she proclaims, "I love you, daddy dear. Mommy, do you love daddy too?"

I must be missing something here because I could swear my wife and daughter just exchanged a conspiratorial glance.

"Yes," replies Sarah, "of course. Will you open the wine, Luc?"

How many years has it been since she's talked to me in that serene tone of voice I used to find so soothing? Is it really too late to start over again? Just as my mind is being invaded by a crazy ray of hope, I suddenly remember that last conversation I had with her shortly before I left the house, or rather was driven from it. As Sarah has so often pointedly remarked, I have no memory. I am incapable of relating exactly what this or that person said, whereas *she* can repeat any conversation in detail, word for word. But what she said to me when she woke up that morning was most revealing, and *those* words have remained embedded in my mind ever since.

Seeing her smile at me in a friendly way, I went to get her coffee, something I hadn't done for quite some time. Then I sat down right next to her.

"What is it, Sarah?"

"Oh, I had the funniest dream."

"Well?"

"You move into some kind of hotel where I already live. At first you're perfectly charming, but then you start making off with all sorts of things I need. The unfortunate part about your room is that everyone's always passing through it." She laughed.

I could feel the blood starting to pound at my temples. Feeling humiliated and disappointed, I rushed into the shower, then raced to the office, slamming the door behind me.

That's just what she's thought of me for quite some time now: I'm a man everyone passes through, an individual whose hazy feelings melt into thin air between two countries guarded by watchtowers.

"My papa," Miriam whispers in my ear, and for a fleeting moment, I suffer from the misleading illusion that everything is as it was before, at the time when José called me *mama*.

Sarah

Someone's just pushed open the door to the yellow bedroom I went up to after dinner. Convinced it's Luc, I stub out my cigarette in the ashtray and turn around.

"Oh, it's *you*."

"Mom, I gotta tell you something. Who're you calling?"

"No one, José."

He leans up against one of the windows, resolutely folds his arms, and watches me put the receiver back on the hook.

"Yeah, right. Everyone in this family is completely out to lunch."

"Except for you, of course. You who pretended to be shooting heroin!"

He shrugs his shoulders, apparently exasperated. "Listen, you can call anyone you want. I really couldn't care less. Christ, it's none of my business anyway."

"In that case, stop bombarding me with questions."

He gives me a dirty look. "She isn't calling anyone," he mutters. "Doesn't that just take the cake."

"If you really must know, I felt like talking to someone normal, someone . . ."

Quick as a flash, he finishes my sentence for me. "Like Erma?"

As a matter of fact, I had completely forgotten about her. Surprised, I stare at my son.

"Why no, of course not. You think I've had time to think about Erma today! I was calling the Master. When I tell him my troubles, he always finds some way to make me laugh."

José's sigh is eloquent. I suppose that, like me, he feels constricted by the tension reigning over the place.

"Mom, why were you so nice to dad at dinner? You were downright syrupy."

I discern an aggressive tone in his voice. He always adored his father, carefully observing his mannerisms and drinking in his words with a rapture that struck me as excessive. When I would see him waiting for Luc at night, face pressed against one of the windows overlooking the street, I got the impression that I counted for nothing. Now that his passion has cooled, he's acting like a jilted lover, never missing an opportunity to trample his father's image.

"Oh, I don't know, José. He's been acting decent today. I'm just trying to do the same. Anyway, you followed me up here. What's so urgent? What is it?"

He shrugs his shoulders. "Nothing."

"José!"

He impatiently gestures to me to sit down. Luc can't abide having serious discussions standing up in what he calls that helter-skelter Abner way. And José is just like him. Perched across from me on a rickety stool, chin in hand, my son asks me: "How do you think Leo's doing?"

"He seems to be doing much better."

"And you think that's all it is?"

How do I explain to him that for more than an hour I have been literally obsessed by that scene Miriam played out for me in Paul's study? If José found out that his father had pressed a gun to his temple, he'd be worried sick.

"I'm relieved that he seems to have pulled himself back together. Billy thought the end was near. He was wrong—and that's that."

"No, mom. He lied."

"What?"

"I'm sure of it, and I'm not the only one who thinks so either."

To tell the truth, when I saw my father beaming at the table just now, his complexion fresh and rosy, a fleeting doubt crossed my mind. But I then became engrossed in the lost, virtually haunted, expression I saw in Luc's eyes and didn't give Leo another thought.

"Wait a minute. You're not insinuating that he never had cancer! No, that I cannot believe. And what about Citrus? Do you imagine that he'd go along with such a morbid conspiracy?"

"They're buddies."

Much as the term *buddy* hardly fits the proper Dr. Citrus, I know he would commit hara-kiri if my father asked him to. As I'm lighting another cigarette, I murmur, "Well, maybe. But why?"

"Grandpa must have his reasons. So what were grandma and grandpa like when you were little, mom? Did they get along?"

I'm suddenly permeated by a deep chill. I begin to shiver.

"Are you playing detective now, José?"

His easygoing attitude notwithstanding, José is stubborn and will not easily relinquish his determination to unravel family mysteries—especially age-old ones. No doubt Jeanne's impending arrival has stirred his curiosity. As tears I cannot manage to hold back come to my eyes, he lays a hand on my arm.

"Don't cry, mom. I didn't mean to upset you. It's just that you've told us lots of stuff about when you were a kid, but you've never told us anything about the two of them together. There's something you don't want to say, isn't there?"

Defeated, I reply, "Yes. Yes, there is. Could you please leave me alone for a minute, my José? With this lump in my throat, I can't ... can't ... Could you please keep dad company?"

"Dad? Why?"

"It would make him happy."

He looks at me, a question on the tip of his tongue, then replies, "Okay, if you say so—and if he doesn't send me packing."

Once the door is again closed, I let myself slide back into the armchair and shut my eyes. A woman appears behind my tightly clenched lids. Her long brown hair is plastered to her face, a face that's as vacant as death . . .

I am little, six years old. It's the middle of December. I know that because there's a big Christmas tree in the middle of the courtyard at school. Its branches are hung with multicolored ornaments and blinking lights. With my fingertips I draw mysterious signs on the icy pane of our bedroom window and look at the black sky swept with frighteningly shaped clouds. Next to me in her crib, my sister cries and cries. I shake a rattle under her nose. I sing her a lullaby. But there is nothing to be done. She is inconsolable. Papa left before dinner. As he was slamming the door, he shouted, "Do whatever you like, Jeanne," and then something else I didn't understand. Mommy made meatballs for me and her, then she rocked Lisa in her arms while I ate my stewed apples. Once again I thought about how she always pays more attention to Zaza than to me. I didn't complain, but I did put my head on her lap. "Tell me one of your stories," she said in her soft voice. "Would you please, treasure?" Yes, she was the one who used to call me *treasure* well before Leo did. So that her eyes wouldn't be so sad, I made up a new episode in the continuing adventures of the Princess with the Little Foot who lives in a kingdom where household objects obey her, and whose only friend is an insolent blabbermouth of a sparrow. I have a talent for telling stories and am very advanced for my age. Everyone tells me so. Later, at the same time she put

Zaza in her crib, I brushed my teeth, got into bed, and must have fallen asleep. What woke me up? Not my sister's crying, but the silence. It's as if the two of us are alone. I put down the rattle and walk out of the room barefoot. "Mommy, mommy?" I whisper, quaking with fear in the darkness. All the lights are out in the apartment. There's only a band of light coming from beneath the bathroom door. "Mommy!" I say louder. And then I hear a sound like running water. I prick up my ears. It's the faucet in the bathtub; maybe mommy's taking a hot bath. I lightly tap at the door twice—no answer. Back in the bedroom, Zaza is screaming louder and louder, and then I knock twice with my clenched fist. It's cold in the hallway. My feet are freezing. I hesitate, then turn the knob and go in. There are red streaks on the tiles of the floor and walls. You'd say, you'd say . . . "No!" I shout, clapping my hands to my chest in a gesture of supplication. "No, no!" My head starts turning from side to side. I stagger. I back out of the room, my toes clinging to the tile. I go downstairs to summon our neighbor, Madame Louise. I don't know where to find the switch to turn on the hall lights, and in the darkness I trip on a stair, then find myself on my knees. A door opens. "Who's there? Come on, answer me." Madame Louise has a gruff voice. "Oh, it's you, Sarah. What are you doing up at this time of night? What's happened to you, dearie?" I try to speak, but my voice won't come out of my throat. She takes me in her arms and gives me a little shake. "Is it upstairs, in your apartment? Look how you're trembling. Did you leave the door open? No? It doesn't matter. I have the key. You can stay here if you want. I'm going up." But I shake my head and follow her. She goes into the bathroom first. "Oh, my God," she exclaims, then puts a fleshy hand over my eyes so I won't look, but it's too late. I've seen my mother with her wrists slashed. The water is red with blood, so much blood. They took her out on a stretcher. Her long hair, which she normally wears pulled back, is plastered to her cheeks, her neck, her bare shoulders. Papa hadn't come back yet, but Madame Louise took care of everything. She went down to her place to get a cot and set it up between me and my sister. "The three of us are going to sleep together, sweetheart." She feels my forehead with her fingers. "I think you have a fever. Now what's the name of your friend the doctor? It's a funny name." She checks the list of names that mommy has tacked to the wall next to the telephone. "Why can't I find it?" "Citrus," I whisper, and she plants a loud kiss on my cheek because I've finally spoken. I've barely finished drinking my hot chocolate when Citrus arrives all out of breath. After he gets me to lie down on the couch and takes my pulse, I start crying so violently that my chest shakes with the sobs. "My darling Sarah," he says, "your mommy's going to get better. You'll see her soon—tomorrow or the day after." But I shiver and answer "No, no," because I don't want to see her any more. I don't want to see her ever again. "Her heart rate is slightly elevated," he murmurs to

Madame Louise. "It's the shock. You can go back home. I'm staying here." "You just wouldn't believe how much I love those two kids, doctor. Sarah is my little ray of sunshine. That little girl is so funny. I just hope that . . . well, you'll let me know if anything happens. I'm not going to sleep a wink all night." She kisses me very hard before leaving. I hear papa's voice coming from the stairs. "What's going on at our house, Madame Louise?" "Your friend the doctor will tell you, Monsieur Abner." Papa rushes over to us. "Where is Jeanne?" he screams. I look at him without moving, but Citrus stands up and puts a hand on papa's shoulder. "Leo," he says softly. "Oh, Leo." Much later, I fall asleep in my father's arms. The next day—I remember it as if it were yesterday—he left Zaza with Madame Louise and took me to the circus, where I cried so much that we had to leave while the trapeze artist was flying through the air. When mama came back home, her hair was once again pulled back—it shone like silk. She had bandages on her wrists, and I couldn't look at her without thinking of her bloody bathwater.

Jeanne left for good a week after she cut open her veins. Lisa doesn't know anything about what happened that night, but I have long felt that if my mother left the three of us, it was my fault for not saying a word to her after she came home from the hospital. Behind my closed eyelids, I again see the dilapidated old rue La Bruyère bathroom, to which I have never been able to return without choking back a wave of nausea. I can't understand why Leo didn't take Lisa and me and move out. Now she's coming back, and I know that, just as in Chicago, before even raising my eyes to meet hers, I will look at the scars crisscrossing her wrists . . .

"Sarah, were you sleeping?"

"No. I was thinking about Jeanne."

He sits down on the stool where José was perched before, and I notice once again just how strong the resemblance is between father and son.

"We have to leave for the station in half an hour. Their train gets in at 11:05."

"Are you the one driving us?"

His voice suddenly turns cold as he answers. "That bother you?"

"No, no, Luc, on the contrary. Who's coming along?"

"If I only knew! Certainly not Paul, in any event. This time he's had more than enough of the Abners."

I smile as I recall the various episodes that have created commotion all day long.

"And what about you, Luc? Have you had enough too?"

He fixes me with his slightly slanted eyes—a throwback to a Mongolian ancestor, according to him.

"Who? Me? I really thought I had. But when all is said and done . . ."

He stands up and, turning his back to me, cracks open the window. I hear him add in a quiet sigh, "I've missed you."

Disturbed by his admission, I absentmindedly flip

through the black notebook I extracted from my purse just now. Today I've hardly written anything down.

"What about the children, Luc?" I ask.

"What about them?"

"Are they coming to the station?"

"José's staying here—I don't think he's in any hurry to see his grandmother—but Miriam's ready to roll right now. As for your sister, she isn't holding up so well."

"Me neither, I'm afraid."

He comes over to me and extends his hand toward my cheek, then quickly restrains himself.

"I know."

When I would criticize him for treating me like a stranger, he would often say, "I know you better than you think, Sarah. It's you who won't let me get close to you."

"I know," he echoes. "But you'll pull through."

"I was thinking about what I saw in the bathroom on rue La Bruyère. No one has the right to do that to a child. Don't you agree?"

He looks away.

"That depends. When you hate yourself, you may prefer no longer imposing yourself on the very people you love most."

His voice is so lifeless it makes me shiver. What has become of the happy-go-lucky social butterfly I knew, the one whose velvety-smooth eye used to linger on other women for so long that I would turn pale with jealousy?

"What! Luc, you don't mean to say that you'd . . ."
He slips his hands into his pockets, then hesitates before replying. "No, no, of course not. I'll be waiting for you downstairs, Sarah."

Luc

The fate of the Abner family used to remind me of a jigsaw puzzle whose pieces, with their strangely distorted shapes, calmly fall back into place on their own, manipulated by chance rather than by any human will. A wife disappears. Ultimately, no one gets too worked up about it—and the family reverts to a seemingly smooth, harmonious circle. But when you have the opportunity I've had to look at this landscape from the inside, you notice that it's bumpier than you thought, and that it is Sarah alone who plugs the gaps while holding the family reins. "Saint Sarah," I would call her, adding, "all you need is a halo." She would then glare at me with her big eyes, for while she may employ her sense of humor at other people's expense, remaining supremely indifferent to their reactions, she hates being teased herself.

And yet I was barely joking, for in raising first Lisa and then our own children, she demonstrated amazing generosity without ever expecting anything in return. Apart from her travails with hair dryers, overnight bags, and dinner parties during which she would give me desperate or imploring looks, panic-stricken at the idea of having to say three words in the presence of people she persisted in labeling *strangers*—apart from all that she's really a good-hearted person in the end. More so now than when I first met her.

On several occasions Erma has asked me to describe Sarah, but I flat out refuse to play that game with someone who'd be hostile to Sarah from the outset. Tonight I get the feeling Sarah senses my despair and unhappiness, and I'm grateful to her for showing me if not love, then at least affection. For once her eyes aren't indifferent, perhaps because she now sees the fissures in my armor—the armor I have donned in recent years just to stand up to her.

Saint Sarah indeed. Inaccessible, impervious to all the rules of the social game—if she even knows them at all, for I'm not convinced she does. She would have liked me to imitate her haughty disdain so that we could live in peace as two marginals. But I was too afraid of floundering in the shadow of her writing. After hesitating, I finally opted for refuge in a universe that, while certainly more prosaic than hers, was also more comforting. The moment I made that decision, she evicted me from her life without the least pity—and I found myself alone in the company of people who meant nothing to me.

In the course of this day, spent in the company of my children and the rest of the Abner tribe, I have been buffeted by contradictory feelings: irritation at finding them unchanged in their complete lack of conformity to the standards of mortal behavior, followed by despair at being excluded from their warm-hearted chaos. Maybe I won't spirit away the revolver in that drawer upstairs after all. Sarah's allusion to Jeanne's failed suicide attempt brought me back to my senses. In any event, I'm returning to Paul's study before going to the station so I can make a phone call without being overheard. And who am I calling? Erma.

"Where're you going, dad?"

José's been tailing me ever since I came downstairs. He's grumpy but clearly intent on not letting me slip away. I've made myself a cup of coffee in the kitchen. He's now sitting next to me leafing through a magazine.

"I've got a call to make."

"Isn't it a little late to be yakking on the phone?"

"No offense, but don't you think that's my business?"

"Well, yeah, I guess," he says with a frown.

"Hey, Joe, are you keeping tabs on me or what?"

Closing his magazine, he replies, "No. I'm keeping you company; there's a difference."

His voice sounds so aggressive I start laughing. He bites his lip, then starts laughing himself.

"Speaking of company, it'd be nice if you came to the station with us. Whaddya say?"

"Maybe. I'm gonna make up my mind at the last minute. After all it *is* true that Jeanne never did anything to me personally."

"So you think she's guilty of something?"

He stares at me dumbfounded. "Of course she is. She flew the coop. Like you, dad."

"But José, I didn't just leave, you know . . ."

"Then what about Erma?"

Defeated, I bow my head. "I felt so lonely. The three of you were together, and I didn't have anyone."

"You had me, dad."

Moved, I look at him. I'd like to ruffle his hair the way I used to, but I don't dare.

"Thanks, José. I should have tried to see you more often."

Once—one single time—I asked Sarah what time he got out of school and I went to wait for him. I felt ill-at-ease standing on a street corner in the middle of all those teenagers. He appeared with Ludo and another boy. He was smiling at his pals as he slipped on his windbreaker. I lit a Camel and noticed that my hands were trembling. José has the most tender, spontaneous smile I know . . . I didn't dare call out or walk up to him. A motorbike came rumbling down the street. At that moment he turned and saw me. He took a few steps back, but I could clearly see his eyes fill with tears. My little boy. Does he know how attached to him I am?

He shrugs his shoulders. "It's nice and peaceful around the house now that you're not there. I just miss you a little on Sunday mornings, that's all. Remember? We used to go running together in the Bois de Vincennes, and afterward we'd bring back croissants for everybody. Now I go running with Ludo, but it's not the same."

"I understand. So . . . let's plan on getting together

next Sunday. *Now* will you let me use the phone? I've barely got ten minutes left."

He shoots me a suspicious look.

"But mom . . ."

I rest my hand on his shoulder.

"Trust me, Joe."

As I'm walking out of the kitchen, I hear Sarah ask Miriam what she's planning to wear to pick up her grandmother. "You're not really going in a nightshirt, are you?"

"Well, I'll put daddy's jacket on over it. If I'm too dressed up, she won't recognize me."

I walk up the stairs as discreetly as possible. As soon as I reach Paul's study, I dial Erma's number. Maybe I'll get her answering machine. That would make matters easier: a simple recorded message.

"Hello."

"It's me."

In the background, I hear what seems to be the Fauré *Requiem*. When I think of all those concerts she dragged me to without ever asking my opinion, I'm amazed at how docile I've been. I'm not even certain if she really likes music—or if it's an affectation she's adopted.

"Yes, Luc."

By chance, or because my voice is so clipped, I'm not entitled to a *sweetie*.

"Listen, Erma, I wanted to tell you not to expect me tomorrow."

Pause. Yes, it *is* the Fauré *Requiem*. I wasn't mistaken.

"You're going to be coming back late. Is that it?"

"I won't be coming back at all. It's over."

"Sarah blackmailed you?"

I can't tolerate it when she utters Sarah's name.

"No! Listen, I have to hang up now."

"Bastard! Have you thought of everything you owe me?"

"I never asked you for a thing."

Bang! She's hung up.

Maxime, my best friend no less, told me after having had dinner with Erma: "I don't get it, pal. All right, fine. I'm mad at Sarah, but what do you see in Erma? She has a side that's . . . oh, I don't know, petty, narrow. It's simple, really: everything about her is small. Anyway, that's your business."

I heave a sigh of relief, leave the study, and walk to the end of the hall. I want to gather my thoughts before rejoining the others. But a noise coming from Paul's study makes me jump. I walk back there, then stop, stunned, in the doorway. In darkness offset only by the yard lights, Sarah is in the process of opening a drawer.

"Sarah?" I whisper.

She gives a cry, then collects herself. "Oh, it's you, Luc."

"What are you doing?" I ask. "Did you follow me?"

"No, no. I was looking for a piece of paper."

She lies so badly that I can't help smiling. In spite of how dark it is, I can see that she's just hidden an object under her jacket. Suddenly I realize that there was a reason for Sarah's kindness, Miriam's outpouring of affection, and José's camaraderie. Someone must have seen me here earlier, maybe one of the children. After turning on the lamp, I hold out my hand to her. "Please hand it over, Sarah."

"So you can use it? Certainly not."

"Please, Sarah. It might be loaded."

I edge cautiously toward her. The revolver bulges beneath her jacket. She folds her arms.

"No. We've had enough accidents in this family."

"Precisely. I'd like to avoid having one more."

Trying not to jostle her, I take another few steps forward and grab the gun, but she fights back, determined not to let go.

"No," she says again in a trembling voice.

Suddenly, as I feared, all hell breaks loose. A shot rings out and bursts right through the window, shattering it.

"Sarah, are you all right?"

"I thought you wanted to . . ." She leans against Paul's desk and bursts into tears. "We're going to be late getting to the station."

"Don't cry, my little kitten," I say.

"Daddy, daddy?"

The rest of them have stampeded up the stairs and

are now rushing into the little study, Miriam first. She leaps into my arms.

"So you're not dead? Mommy saved your life?"

"If you like."

Leo sits on the sofa next to Lisa. Eyes creased in thought, he surveys us both. As for Paul, he's standing with his head in his hands, rocking back and forth. If there's one person certain to retain an indelible memory of this weekend, it's him.

"Mom, dad, did you have a fight?" asks José as he sticks his hand through the broken pane.

Even though his tone is nonchalant, Sarah shoots me an anxious look.

"I'll explain later, José," I say levelly in an effort to be reassuring. "Right now, however, it's time for us to hit the road. Come on, let's get a move on. Leo, are you coming?"

"I don't know," my father-in-law replies abruptly.

"What, papa?" exclaims Sarah. "Are you joking?"

"No, treasure, I'm terrified. My legs have turned to jelly."

"He can simply stay here with me and Adeline," Paul offers weakly. "Now that you've had every possible accident and staged every conceivable dramatic episode, we need no longer be excessively worried— and perhaps the three of us can sip a nightcap in peace while waiting."

"Leo," Sarah says firmly as she takes her father by the arm, "Jeanne has traveled all the way from Chicago just for you. You have to come."

When we finally finish going down the stairs single file, I suddenly realize that someone is missing: Paul's lodger Billy, the amnesiac.

"Where is Billy?" bellows Miriam, as if reading my thoughts. "Is he coming to the station too?"

"No, darling. There's no room in my car."

"Too bad," she replies. "He's so funny."

But downstairs, a man is crouched a few feet away from my brand-new Ford examining the pieces of broken glass.

"Murder at Echards," he murmurs in that irritating accent of his. "In a novel, I'd be the gardener with a secret nobody knows. Do you not like me, Luc?"

"No, I do not."

"Well, that makes us even, then."

On the way to the station, Lisa is seized by a coughing fit. In my rearview mirror, I see José give her several vigorous slaps on the back.

"Don't bother," she whispers. "It's stronger than I am. Apparently I'm the only one among you who won't recognize her. My own mother."

The train is just pulling into the station as we reach the platform. I cast a quick glance at my cargo. Sarah, who's holding a bouquet of anemones in one hand, has slipped her free hand around the shoulders of her now deathly pale sister. The children are staring wide-eyed at the train. Standing slightly off to one side, Leo puts his flask to his mouth, then wipes his lips with the back of his hand.

As I observe them, I also think of the improbable,

typically Abnerian tale I heard just now from my son's mouth: Leo, heroic Leo, the man for whom the truth is a historical necessity, as he would say—this same Leo is supposed to have fabricated his liver cancer for the sole purpose of bringing Jeanne back.

"Sorry to disappoint you, Joe," I said to my son before we got in the car, "but I saw the test results myself."

"So he's really going to die?"

"In all likelihood."

Nodding his head a bit sadly, he murmured, "Well, at least he wasn't lying."

At the very moment the train stops, Miriam—strangely arrayed in my leather jacket over her night-shirt, which is flapping at her ankles—starts running back and forth along the platform.

"I see them, I see them. C'mon, mom, give me the flowers—I *am* the littlest, you know!"

She has already come up to Citrus, who has descended first and is now offering his hand to the woman I met in Paris. As the two of them slowly wend their way toward us, I am suddenly put in mind of a passage from Zoro, the routine that Sarah wrote.

"My mother came back from the camps in her striped pajamas. She was in a very good mood. 'I really think the ovens should be electric,' she said, 'because gas, well, gas is a little dangerous.' "

But Jeanne is coming back from exile, not from the camps. When she settles her big, affectionate eyes upon us, I am gripped by a wave of emotion that I am unable to control. Next to me, I can feel Sarah trembling as well.

"Mama," murmurs Lisa, "you're here!"

And as a mild breeze sweeps the platform, Leo stands before his wife, his white head bowed, and bursts into heartrending sobs.

Sarah

While the train carrying Jeanne and Citrus rolls toward us at a rapid pace, I am also engaging in a journey. A landscape made up of randomly commingled memories is flashing before my attentive eyes at a dizzying speed. My unfortunate mother left quite a long time ago, hiding her injured wrists far away from us. When she appears before me, she will ask nothing of me. I know that, but I will feel obliged to give her an accounting. For in her absence—even if I have long refused to admit it—I'm the one who has served as a guide to my crippled family.

I'm worried about Lisa, as usual. I was six years old when Leo, my sister, and I were abandoned. I was, of course, too young to take Jeanne's place in the life of a one-year-old baby. And yet I already showed signs of a certain authoritativeness. I was the one who taught Lisa how to use a toilet. Even if my methods were hardly conventional—indeed, I would go so far as to term them extremely fanciful—one fine day I was able to tell my father proudly: "Zaza is toilet-trained, papa. She won't be needing diapers or baby pants any more. That stuff is over."

But the year I started junior high school was when

I really became a substitute mother to my sister. I taught her to read and did such a good job that after one month of grade school, she could read as ably as any adult. I also set up play dates for her when she didn't have school, making arrangements on an equal footing with her classmates' mothers, and I took her to her piano lessons Tuesday nights. When she had done well, I'd buy her a chocolate eclair or, greatest reward of all, take her to see an American movie since she was learning English from my textbook as fast as I was.

Sometimes, seeing that I was having a hard time keeping my eyes open at night, Leo would ask me: "Are you sure you're not pushing yourself too hard, treasure? I've told you a thousand times that the factory's doing well and I can hire someone to take care of Zaza any time."

"No, Leo," I would protest vehemently. "I don't need anyone."

And my father would scour me with his piercing gaze, probably understanding better than I what I was trying to prove. By taking so much responsibility for Lisa's upbringing, I was escaping the wound Jeanne's leaving had inflicted on me. The gap was plugged. There had been no tragedy in our family. And we were living like normal people.

Even if I took care of my sister in a way that verged on the obsessive, I still had energy and imagination to spare. Because I was bored to death in school, I would work off my frustrations by cooking up schemes— sometimes alone, sometimes with my classmates—in the most questionable taste. That business with the pornographic letters gives some idea of the style of my devilish inventions. Of course, while I considered myself a supreme wit, Leo was tearing his hair and praying in Hebrew to Elohim for help. (When all else fails, my father becomes a believer.) But Elohim, probably figuring that he didn't have to bother himself with the prayers of an intermittent believer, remained silent, and my pranks continued unabated.

My father was no doubt awaiting with terror my entry into adolescence. He must have thought I'd stay out all night every night and slide, as the neighbors on our floor had predicted, into a life of wanton depravity. But in truth, it was just the opposite. Around boys, I suffered from an acute shyness that I hid beneath an air of detachment and ridicule. I came home punctually every night to rue La Bruyère, helped Lisa do her homework, listened to Leo's friends discuss politics, and—once everyone had left—wrote in my bed until the wee hours of the morning. When I successfully completed high school, Leo's anxieties faded away. He must have counted himself lucky to have two healthy, well-balanced daughters.

But here he had gone and forgotten—as had I, for that matter—that Lisa too would grow up one day. Until then, she had been nestled under my protective wing. And whereas I, although shy, spontaneously said whatever came into my head, my sister remained silent most of the time, content to observe. What's more, unlike me, she hated being noticed. Leo's exuberance drove her to distraction, and she found my incisive observations annoying. Apart from her running away on occasion, there was no reason to suspect she wouldn't renounce childhood peacefully, without causing the least stir. But when I discovered that Lisa, then fourteen years old, had a boyfriend who was in medical school, the scales fell from my eyes.

"At least you haven't slept with him, Zaza."

"Sure I have," she replied calmly.

"What? But you'll get pregnant. Are you crazy?"

"Don't worry. He wore a rubber."

"Thank God . . . I guess. So how . . . how was it?"

"Not so great. Besides, I'm going to dump him."

A demonic cycle was beginning. After going through a disturbingly rapid succession of casual boyfriends, she had her heart broken for the first time, which upset her so much that she swallowed that plant fertilizer. Then she went through a homosexual period. And far from hiding anything from me, she told me of her experiences in a perfectly matter-of-fact way.

"I'm glad," Leo told me one day in an ironic tone I didn't catch at the time, "that your sister is less antisocial than you are. The telephone rings for her nonstop. Have you noticed?"

I curtly replied that *yes*, I *had* noticed. But the worst was still to come. At the time my first novel was published, the only one of them ever to make anyone cry, I experienced a kind of giddiness and paid less attention to the racy soap opera that was Lisa's love life. One afternoon as I was roughing out a comic monologue for the Master, Lisa came home looking bright and chipper. She gave me a loud kiss on the cheek, then sat down across from me.

"Am I bothering you, Sarah?"

"No, it's okay. I'm just looking for ideas."

"More horrors about ovens and camps, the all-but-anti-Semitic and the more-than-Jewish? Basically, you have it in for everybody."

"Not *me*, Zaza. My *boss*."

"Your boss, my foot! Birds of a feather flock together. Want some tea?"

Whenever she offered to make me tea, it meant she wanted to talk. I had only to wait.

"We saw your book in a store window."

"What do you mean, *we*?"

"Sarah, don't look at me like that. A man and I."

Concluding that her homosexual phase had come to an end, I asked: "Who is it?"

Her cheeks flushed bright pink. She sighed.

"You're gonna squawk. I know you. You're worse than a mother hen."

"Is he as awful as all that?"

"No. It's just that he's a friend of Leo's."

I shivered.

"Which one? Come on, Zaza! Which one?"

"He only came over here once. You know, the one who would eat only goulash."

"*That* guy? Why, to begin with, he's thirty years older than you are, and what's more, he's hideous looking. Dracula in the flesh!"

"He's very cultured. A change of pace, if you like. Anyway, he's invited me to spend next weekend with him in his place on the outskirts of town."

"Oh, Lisa, you're out of your mind. He's the kind of person you run away from as fast as you can. You couldn't seriously consider spending the weekend with him."

"Maybe *you* couldn't," she tossed off as she stood up, "but *I'm* going."

When Leo came home from the factory, I asked him offhandedly how intimately he knew his friend who ate only goulash. My father rolled his eyes.

"You mean Shoura? He's no friend. I can't even remember who brought him to our house. In any event, he's half crazy. He was suspected of having murdered his wife, but the police were never able to prove it."

That night I went through my sister's purse looking for her new suitor's address. Upon finding it, I promised myself that I would snatch her from the clutches of the horrid Shoura. The following Saturday night around eight, I settled behind the wheel of my beat-up old Citroën and, after winding through the twisting streets of a seedy suburb, finally pulled up to Shoura's house. I had to ring several times—I remember that clearly. He finally appeared, decked out in a long white robe.

"What do you want?"

"I'm Lisa's sister. I've come to get her."

"Sorry, she's not here."

He then tried to shut the door, but I stuck my foot in it.

"If you don't let me in, I'm coming back with the cops."

He gave me a sidelong glance, then opened the door with a shrug.

"As you like, Mademoiselle Abner, but your sister came to my house of her own accord."

As I walked in, I immediately saw two candles on a table set for one, but no trace of Lisa.

"Where is she?"

A bloodcurdling scream then rang out, shaking the whole house. I ran up the stairs two at a time with Shoura right behind me and emerged into a room lit solely by the flame of another candle, only to come upon a dreadful scene: my poor Zaza naked and blindfolded and bound to some sort of board.

While standing there petrified, wondering what to do, I noticed a kitchen knife lying on a table. When my sister screamed again, I said very clearly, "I'm here, Zaza. Don't be scared."

But that horrible man had grabbed my arm and twisted it so far that I almost fainted from the pain. I stomped on his foot as hard as I could, then snatched up the knife as he reeled backward, shut my eyes, and drove the blade into his chest where I thought his heart was located. While Shoura, moaning grotesquely, collapsed to the floor, I freed my little sister, whose teeth were chattering in panic. Then I helped her back into her clothes and drove her home. I had hoped that Leo would be asleep already, but the moment I opened the door, the acrid smell of his cigar tickled my nose.

"Sarah, don't tell him anything," Lisa whispered to me imploringly.

Our father was sitting in the armchair next to the window, a book closed on his lap. He looked at us without saying a word.

"Zaza's not feeling well, Leo. I'm going to help her get to bed."

He leaned his head toward the window and kept still. I gave my sister a tranquilizer. Once she was in bed, I took her in my arms and whispered, "Sleep now, darling. Everything will be better in the morning."

She opened her mouth to say something, then gave up and fell asleep.

When I came back down to the living room, Leo was kneeling in front of the liquor cabinet.

"You aren't going to bed, papa?"

"No, not yet."

He turned around.

"Here, Sarah, drink this glass of cognac. Judging by how pale you are, I imagine you need it."

"Yes, I sure do. Listen, Leo, we . . . we went out to dinner together and witnessed a pretty gruesome accident on the street."

"Don't bother lying, treasure. Shoura called me an hour ago to tell me that you had tried to kill him. Too bad you didn't succeed."

All of a sudden my nerves snapped and I burst into uncontrollable waves of mad laughter.

"I couldn't remember if the heart was on the right

or the left. Next time I want to kill someone, I'll have to brush up on my anatomy first."

My father flashed me a smile.

"My poor darling. I never should have left you to take care of your sister alone."

"So you know the whole story, papa?"

He nodded his head sadly.

"Yes, from the very beginning I've always known everything about Lisa: the affairs with the men, the affairs with the women . . . all of it. You're the educated one in this family. How do you explain it?"

I see my little sister as a child again; she's so calm, so orderly, never raises her voice.

"I think it's a way for her to keep from thinking. It's as if she's running away, the way she did when she was little. Because she has no memory of Jeanne, she lacks a solid foundation to which she can attach herself. She's looking for something but doesn't know exactly what it is—maybe nothing more than human warmth."

Leo stubbed out his cigar, then uttered this mysterious phrase: "When you know the truth, will you forgive me, Sarah?"

I'm sitting in Luc's Ford between my two children. Lisa is coughing like there's no tomorrow, and I have to restrain myself from yelling at her to stop. All these years I've made an effort to spare her feelings and never cause her pain, but now my assignment is coming to an end, for our mother is coming to relieve me. Maybe when my sister sees for herself those wrists crisscrossed with scars, she will finally understand that Jeanne committed no crime.

It was that absurd scene we just played out in Paul's study that reminded me of the sordid night when I almost became a murderer to save Zaza. Of course I turned that nightmare into a juicy anecdote, and Luc laughed his head off when I told it to him.

"Sarah," he said, "I've always suspected you were capable of killing someone in a fit of rage."

"Only to protect those I love," I protested.

He then settled those alluring eyes of his on me and said, "Why, you'd kill even me without the least bit of remorse if I made you too unhappy."

He was right in the end. When he would turn his back to me at night, taking refuge in sleep after one of our fights, I'd sometimes get a burning desire to strangle him.

"Mommy?"

"What, sweetheart?"

"Mommy, are you happy to be seeing *your* mommy?"

Luc's eye catches mine in the rearview mirror.

"Yes," I reply a bit coolly. "Of course I am."

It's raining as we pull up to the station. Leo extricates himself from the car with great difficulty. While everyone was getting ready, Luc found the time to tell me that Leo had indeed been stricken with cancer.

"I know that José and Paul have managed to convince themselves that he fabricated the whole story, but he's telling the truth—Citrus showed me the lab reports. I'm sorry, Sarah. I love Leo too," he said, then pressed his lips to my forehead.

Was it raining the day she left? It was in December, shortly before Christmas. Was it mere coincidence that when I went to visit her, it was also during the Christmas season? She had a little tree draped with multicolored tinsel in the middle of her living room and we ate a turkey, just the two of us.

On the platform, my eyes are misting over, and I have to make an effort to stay upright. Miriam is running around and Leo has moved away from us, but Luc, José, Lisa, and I form a tight little group. Miriam shouts something. I make out Citrus. And then there she is, walking slowly toward us. She's standing up very straight, her hair pulled back as usual, but I can't make out her expression. When she used to come pick me up at school, I was proud because she was prettier than the other mommies. Perhaps for the last time, Lisa clings to me.

"Don't be scared," I murmur. "Don't be scared, Zaza."

Jeanne first goes up to Leo, who is all curled in on himself. Then, with her granddaughter's hand in hers, she grasps my father's hand and joins it to their two clasped hands. All she says is: "Leo."

And when the man she left so long ago starts crying, I can no longer keep back my own tears. Lisa finally releases my arm and takes a step toward them—our parents. I wonder what she's going to do. Slap

Jeanne? Insult her? But instead I hear her gasp in a voice from days gone by, her little girl voice, "Mama, you're here."

Then she throws out her arms and embraces Jeanne as hard as she can.

"Mama," she says again. "Oh, mama."

On that anonymous platform, my mother kisses us one after the other before stopping in front of José.

"May I give you a kiss too?" she asks.

"Yes, grandmother," our son replies. "I'm glad you're here."

No one has thought to say hello to Citrus, who is standing off to one side, overcome with emotion. I go over to him, my cheeks still damp with tears and, taking his hands in mine, murmur, "Thank you. You've done a good deed here."

He bows his head by way of acknowledgment.

"Let's get going," shouts Luc. "It's starting to pour. Everybody in the car. I'll load you all in."

Because there are so many of us, the children crouch in the back of the station wagon. After first protesting, Leo sits in front, and my mother, finding herself between her two daughters, reaches out her arms and draws us to her. As her special scent envelops me—"Mama," I used to say, "I want to smell nice like you"—I realize that only now have my thoughts turned to her wrists. No doubt I forgave her for that long ago.

"Are you going to live with us?" shouts Miriam.

My mother's luminous eyes settle on Leo's profile.

"I do not think so, dear. If your grandfather will have me, I am going to move in with him."

Leo finally turns around. He has drawn his flask from his pocket, but his hand is trembling. I sense that he doesn't dare confront the direct gaze of the woman he allowed to leave so many years ago.

"Yes," he says in an unsteady voice, "Jeanne is coming back home to rue La Bruyère."

"And what about you, daddy?" our daughter again asks. "Are you coming home?"

"I don't know, Miriam," Luc replies.

"Because you can bring E with you, you know—that's his companion, grandma. We'll keep her in a corner of the living room and take her out for a walk every day so she can get some fresh air."

At that point, as the Ford is turning up the drive leading to Echards, everyone bursts out laughing, Luc first.

As my mother is murmuring "I have missed you so much, my darling daughters," I make out Paul's silhouette on the front porch.

And hearing her say *my darling daughters* in her warm voice, I again see the two of us eating our meatballs on those nights when Leo would leave, slamming the door behind him. And I remember the stories I would make up so I could see her smile at me.

Béatrice Shalit has worked as a TV producer in Nigeria and France. She has also written radio plays, as well as the screenplay for *Lisa, Lisa* (her fifth novel).